I dedicate my first novel to Ruth Davis, my seventh grade English teacher. Mrs. Davis was the first to recognize my gift and affirm my passion for writing. I have had no contact with Mrs. Davis in the forty-seven years since middle school (and feel sure she would have no recollection of me as a student), but I will always remember and cherish her influence and inspiration.

Phoebe Stephens
2015

Diary in the Attic

by

Cindy L. Freeman

Cindy L. Freeman

DORRANCE PUBLISHING CO., INC.
PITTSBURGH, PENNSYLVANIA 15222

This is a work of fiction. Names, characters, places, and incidents are either the product of the author's imagination or are used fictitiously, and any resemblance to actual persons, living or dead; events; or locales is entirely coincidental.

ISBN: 978-1-4349-0756-1
Printed in the United States of America

First Printing

For more information or to order additional books, please contact:
Dorrance Publishing Co., Inc.
701 Smithfield Street
Pittsburgh, Pennsylvania 15222
U.S.A.
1-800-788-7654
www.dorrancebookstore.com

Chapter 1

It had been a long, frantically busy week. Margaret couldn't wait to get home and sink every aching muscle into a luxurious bubble bath. As she entered the kitchen through the garage door, she absentmindedly dropped her car keys on the nearest counter and walked out of her backless pumps, tossing her coat on the nearest chair. From upstairs, her spa tub was calling, but first she would pour a generous glass of wine. Finally, as she submerged up to her chin in warm, soothing bubbles, the events of the day came flooding back.

"How could I have been so stupid?" she wondered aloud. The sound of her own voice, echoing on the bathroom tiles, startled her. Margaret had grown accustomed to solitude these past few months—she actually enjoyed being alone—but she sometimes surprised herself with the sound of her own voice. *I promised myself I wouldn't let that witch get to me again*, she continued (this time inside her head). *I can't believe I let her have power over me again, especially after the last time!*

The "witch" was Corinne Melton, a colleague at Beeston Design Firm. Corinne was one of those difficult people who succeeded in creating a tense atmosphere whenever she entered a room. She seemed to carry a chip on her shoulder that even Margaret—who usually relished a challenge—couldn't motivate herself to tackle. Corinne was so defensive and unpleasant that she just wasn't worth the effort.

Okay, that's the last time! Margaret resolved, anew. *From now on, I'll simply avoid her. I'll be cordial but distant.*

Between sudsy caresses of the lavender-scented bubbles and sips of her favorite brand of Riesling, she was finally beginning to relax when the phone rang. *Nothing is getting me out of this tub until the water goes cold and my toes turn into prunes*, she decided and let it ring.

If it's important, the caller will leave a message. I may not even check my messages until morning. My Friday evenings belong to me, she defended a few minutes later, as she slipped into her favorite fleece robe and fuzzy slipper socks and prepared to watch an old movie in bed. Anticipation of this relaxing ritual held the power to motivate her even through the toughest week. She would skip dinner, opting instead for a bowl of popcorn or Wheat Thins—maybe an apple cut into wedges—and a cup of steaming herbal tea.

Once more in the kitchen, Margaret placed a mug of water in the microwave and grabbed a paring knife from the drawer. She noticed the blinking light on the wall phone and remembered the earlier call. Normally, she would have ignored it. All of her closest friends were acquainted with her "regal routine," as they dubbed it (with noses in the air for effect). Months ago, they had given up inviting her out on Friday evenings, and while they teased her about the self-imposed isolation, they had come to respect her wishes.

Tonight, however, something drew her to the phone. *…Probably just one of those election campaign messages*, she speculated. *Once I'm settled in bed, I'll listen to it. At least then, I can erase it, and that annoying blinking will stop. The movie doesn't start for another hour, anyway.* The old classics were her favorites, and tonight's feature was "Bringing Up Baby" with Cary Grant and Katherine Hepburn. Margaret had seen it at least a dozen times since childhood, but she never tired of the perfectly executed comic antics of those two legendary actors.

She returned upstairs to her bedroom and raised a window slightly. A gentle, cool breeze swept past her, carrying with it the sweet scent of something beginning to bloom in her neighbor's yard. Finally, she nestled among more-than-enough fluffy pillows with her "Friday feast" tray balanced on her lap. A few Christmases ago, her mother had given her a bamboo breakfast tray. At the time she thought it a strange and useless gift, but as always, Mom seemed to sense what she needed before any notion occurred to her eldest child.

Just as she reached for the phone, nearly dousing her comforter with hot tea, the doorbell rang. *Who could that be?* she wondered, deciding to pretend she wasn't home. None of her *real* friends would dare interrupt her sacred rite, but now-frantic-sounding knocks accompanied the incessant ringing.

"I'm coming!" she finally announced with exasperation. Setting the tray aside, she jumped out of bed, grabbing her robe at the exact moment her feet touched the plush bedside rug. The phone slid off the satin coverlet and landed on the wooden floor with a crash. She bent to retrieve it with one hand while attempting to tie her sash with the other, but before accomplishing either task, her attention diverted, again, to the front door, where now she could hear a voice. Someone was calling her name. The urgency of the voice sent shivers up and down her spine. Her heart began to race, and suddenly her hands were shaking. By the time she stumbled to the bottom of the stairs, she recognized the voice as Sara's.

"What in the…?" she began, as she quickly unlocked the door and flung it open. "What's going on?" Her voice sounded irritated, but at this point, fear replaced her initial annoyance.

Sara, a co-worker and her best friend, was well aware that Margaret didn't accept callers on Friday evenings. Only something urgent would have brought her to Margaret's front door. "Maggie, you have to come! I told them you wouldn't answer your phone. I said you probably wouldn't even check your messages until morning!"

Sara was talking too fast and too loud, ignoring Margaret's attempts to interrupt her with pleas of "Told whom?" "Come where?" and "What's happened?"

Finally, Margaret grabbed Sara's shoulders firmly, and the ranting subsided as both women drew a deep breath together. "Now, tell me what's going on?"

"It's Corinne," Sara finally managed to say, beginning to cry.

"Corinne?" Margaret blurted, disgust filling her voice. "Accident? What kind of accident?"

"Car accident. She's in the hospital. It's really bad, Maggie! She's really…!" Sara was sobbing. "She's dying. The doctor said she probably won't make it through the night."

Margaret stood frozen, trying to absorb the words that broke through her friend's uncharacteristic sobs. "She's calling for you, Maggie. She wants to see you—only *you*!"

"Me? Why me?"

"I don't know. Just hurry and get dressed. You have to come!"

"All right, but please calm down!" Margaret called, already bounding up the stairs. "I don't want a raving lunatic driving me to the hospital!"

As Sara paced back and forth in the foyer, fumbling with her car keys and trying to calm her frazzled nerves, her friend was pulling a pair of jeans out of the hamper. From the window seat where she had tossed it earlier, Margaret grabbed the blouse that she had worn to work that day, and she slipped on the same jeans and blouse, not even noticing that she wasn't wearing a bra. Her mind was racing. *What could Corinne possibly want with me? Why would she be calling my name on her deathbed? Deathbed! Oh, my God! This is incredible!*

Chapter 2

Margaret had seen her grandmother die, but the woman was in her eighties. Surprisingly, it had turned out to be a heartwarming experience. The whole family had gathered at the spacious farmhouse in central Pennsylvania. There was enough warning of her impending death that even the most distant relatives were able to get there in time to say a proper "good-bye." Margaret, her parents, and her brother Jim had arrived late the previous night after driving five hours through a blinding snowstorm—the worst in twenty years, as it turned out. Others barely made it in time because of cancelled or delayed flights.

Margaret was in high school at the time, and although she adored Grandma Monroe, her initial reaction was more of annoyance than sadness. She would be missing the last football game of the season, and the dance…well, she had finally gotten hunky quarterback Zach Mitchell's attention, and he had asked her to go with him. Instead, that hussy cheerleader, Laurie Thompson, got the chance to make her move.

When the news came, Zach had already been in the locker room, suiting up for the big game. Margaret sent her brother Jim to tell him, taking a big risk that Jim might concoct some harebrained story to sabotage any possibility of a future relationship with Zach. Under normal circumstances, Jim would have done anything to annoy his older sister, but this was different. Their grandmother was dying. Maybe it was the tone of their father's voice or the distant, forlorn look in his eyes as he broke the news to his children, but somehow Jim sensed that this was one of life's experiences to treat with reverence.

After delivering his message, Jim reported that Zach "took the news like a man," sent his well wishes, and said he would call Margaret on Monday. At least he wasn't angry. He seemed to understand that this situation was beyond Margaret's control.

Margaret's family had been nearly the last to arrive at the farmhouse that night. It wasn't like the traditional Thanksgiving or Christmas gathering, filled with excited greetings, sumptuous kitchen smells, and noisy chatter. Rather, the atmosphere was somber, the greetings, warm but subdued, and the conversations, hushed. Margaret recalled feeling afraid to see her beloved Grandma. She wanted to remember her as the vibrant, active, nurturing woman who had always been the rock-solid matriarch of the family—the woman whom she assumed would live forever.

Memories of glorious, carefree summers spent in the stately country house, furnished with antiques and decorated with Grandma Monroe's impeccable sense of style, flooded over her, and she had to hold back tears that threatened to spill onto the well-worn Persian carpet. Forgotten then were the game, the dance, and even Zach Mitchell.

Olivia Monroe (who stood no taller than five feet and seldom exceeded one hundred pounds) had been a larger-than-life kind of woman. Margaret dearly loved and deeply admired her. Despite being one of six grandchildren, Margaret always felt special to her grandma. Jim never wanted to join her month-long summer visits, preferring to stay home and help their dad with the lumber business. Playing baseball also occupied his time and held his attention. Margaret, however, counted the days until she could board the Amtrak and settle in with a good "read" and a thermos of ice-cold lemonade. By the time she was twelve, her parents felt comfortable sending her alone. After all, there were no stops or layovers, and Grandpa Monroe would be waiting for her at the station. Margaret felt very grown up and not at all afraid of traveling alone. She hadn't learned until recently that the railway personnel had always been alerted in advance by her parents, and the conductors were watchful. She remembered only one incident of unwanted attention.

A well-dressed man carrying a leather briefcase took the window seat facing hers. She glanced fleetingly at him but continued reading. After a few minutes, she noticed him staring at her with the faintest hint of a smirk on his face. Feeling a vague sense of discomfort, Margaret raised her book so that it covered her face and shifted nervously in her seat. She wasn't sure why, but she was beginning to feel agitated, as if a mild electric shock coursed through her body. It was a new sensation, one that caused her to feel like running away. Had there been an empty seat, she would have moved, but the car was full, except for the two aisle seats beside her and the stranger. Her backpack occupied one, and his briefcase, the other. Convincing herself that she was overreacting, she, again, shifted her position and settled into a new chapter, finally losing herself in the riveting plot.

"...Must be a good book!"

Margaret jumped visibly, startled by the sudden comment.

"Uh huh," she responded, not wanting to be rude but trying not to sound interested in starting a conversation. Ordinarily, she was friendly and outgoing, but something about this man made the hairs on the nape of her neck stand at attention. She kept her eyes on the page, but was no longer reading.

"So, where are you headed, little lady?" the stranger continued.

"Harrisburg," she answered curtly.

"All alone?"

"Um hum."

"...Mighty long trip for a young girl by herself."

"It's not that far," she answered, dryly, with panic beginning to creep into her voice. Margaret realized the man did not intend to leave her to her reading and wondered how she would escape this uncomfortable predicament. She suspected that, if she headed to the dining car, he would follow her. A trip to the restroom would provide only temporary respite, but it might afford her time to form a plan. As Margaret reached for her backpack, the man quickly, but clumsily, shifted to the vacant seat beside her. It was then that she recognized an all-too-familiar odor on his breath. She remembered the same sickening smell from Great Uncle Edwin. The last time she saw him, she had been only six, but she never forgot that smell, the wild look in his eyes, or his too-affectionate hugs.

"So, little lady..." the stranger began, leaning into her shoulder. Those, however, were the last words she heard him speak. The conductor (who had been observing for a few minutes) appeared, suddenly, and was standing over them.

"Mr. Pierce, come with me please!" he ordered, instantly taking the man by the arm. "You've been upgraded to First Class. Come along. I have a seat for you right through here, sir." There was no time to argue or resist this firm but cheerful command. The man went without incident, seeming, instantly, to forget about the "little lady."

Shaken, but relieved and grateful, Margaret took a deep breath, returned her backpack to the vacated seat, and completed her trip uneventfully. She never saw Mr. Pierce again, and she never mentioned the incident to her parents, fearing that they might curtail any future unaccompanied trips. But, she never forgot the powerful sensation of "fight or flight" induced by the incident and learned to trust this innate survival instinct.

Chapter 3

Sara was rambling as she drove her friend to the hospital. "Nobody knows how it happened. She was alone in the car, and evidently, no other vehicles were involved. The cop said she just ran off the road and hit a tree."

Margaret's alter ego was thinking, *That's what she gets for being nasty to everybody*, but she silenced the thought as quickly as it surfaced, knowing full well that no one deserves to die this way.

"But why would she ask for me? You don't suppose she blames me. Oh, my God, Sara, you don't suppose she blames me for the accident, do you? She could be laying a curse on me right now!"

"Don't be ridiculous, Maggie!"

"But…" Margaret was beginning to panic. "I know she hates me, and we had that huge argument yesterday. I was determined to have the last word—for a change. For once, I stood up to her and now this! What am I going to say to her? Does she look horrible?"

"No, that's the weird part. She has a bruise on her forehead and a couple of scratches, but nothing else visible. I heard two nurses talking outside her room. One of them mentioned 'massive internal injuries.'"

"This is a nightmare!" Margaret cried, intermittently holding her face in her hands. "What about her family? Have they been called?"

"The hospital staff can't seem to locate anyone."

"Who called you?" Margaret asked, consciously trying to calm her frayed nerves with deep breathing.

"Jonathan. He's waiting at the hospital."

Jonathan Craig was their boss at Beeston. He had worked there for nearly twenty-five years and was well respected and highly competent. Margaret had only one previous supervisor with whom to compare him, but she thought Jonathan embodied the ideal boss. He was consistently respectful of all employees—from the maintenance crew to the president of the company. Not that Margaret had ever met the president, but she could envision Jonathan treating him no differently than any of his employees.

Although, clearly, Jonathan was old enough to be her father—in fact, his two children were nearly her age—she found him quite attractive…his fit physique, his full head of salt-and-pepper hair, and the confident way he carried himself. She would have to describe him as distinguished looking. Her main attraction, however, was to his calm, yet authoritative manner. He had a way of leading without dominating. His staff meetings were efficient and effective, and with the exception of Corinne, his staff shared a sense of collegiality.

Work could be hectic and stressful at times, but Margaret loved the teamwork aspect of her job as much as she adored being an interior designer. After only a few months at Beeston, she was convinced that she had found her calling. She also relished living in a small town again, where she could actually afford to own a home. Apartment living in New York had been an exciting way to start a career, but she was a small town girl at heart.

Apart from living paycheck to paycheck and never feeling entirely safe in the city, she longed for a slower pace, and after the heart-rending breakup with Ned Romney, she jumped at the chance to move away and start life afresh: new job, new house (new to her, anyway), and hopefully, new friendships. Eventually, there would be a new boyfriend, but for the time being, she was perfectly content with her self-imposed single life. Both new relationships and new jobs required time and energy, and besides, Margaret just wasn't ready for another commitment. Several men had asked her out within the past two years. She even agreed, reluctantly, to one date, but the protective emotional wall she had built around herself since Ned kept most men at a safe distance. She would not allow herself to be that vulnerable again…not until she felt sure it was the real deal.

Margaret had never liked dating around. It made her feel cheap. She longed to settle down with a good, stable, adoring husband and start a family. Because playing the field wasn't her style, for the time being, she would socialize in groups, cultivate female friendships, and trust that her soul mate would come along when the time was right. A recurring dream about being middle-aged and alone plagued her from time to time, but she tried not to take it seriously during waking hours.

Chapter 4

The last five minutes of Sara's discourse had been wasted on her passenger, but Margaret abruptly snapped out of her trance when Sara nearly shouted, "Maggie, you need to help me find a parking place!" The sky had begun to grow dark, and it was raining.

"Okay, okay!" she answered, not meaning to sound terse. "I think we'll have to try the parking garage. I don't see anything on the street." She hadn't even noticed when the hospital came into view, despite the huge, red *Emergency Room* sign directly in front of her. Her mind had been flitting from one thought to another. Curiosity was now beginning to replace her initial anxiety and subsequent dread. "Why would Corinne want to see me? Maybe she's out of her mind—hallucinatory—she probably suffered a concussion."

Sara pulled into the underground garage and managed to find a space near the elevator. "Intensive Care is on the fourth floor. Come on," she urged as they stepped out of the car and entered the empty elevator.

"What if she's dead already, Sara? What if she wanted to apologize...to ask my forgiveness? What if I never know why she called for me?"

"What if! What if!" mocked Sara. "Let's just calm down and take one step at a time."

"Look who's talking about calming down," answered Margaret, sarcastically.

Then, as if struck by lightning, Sara swung around to face her friend. There was strange clarity in her eyes as she turned Margaret's shoulders so that their gazes met. "Maggie, it's possible that we're the last people—that *you* are the last person—Corinne will see on this earth."

Before Margaret could respond, the elevator stopped with a jerk at the fourth floor of the hospital where Corinne Melton, age twenty-seven, lay dying.

Chapter 5

Death, Margaret had discovered at an early age, was as spiritual
an experience as birth, marriage, or any of life's passages. To be
present at the death of a loved one was a rare privilege—a blessing
even. Of course, she would miss Grandma Monroe. The loss
would affect her for a lifetime, but the actual moment of death,
when Grandma opened her eyes and looked upward, filled
Margaret with awe. She would never know what Olivia Monroe
saw in that instant, but whatever it was washed her with total
peace. For an instant, her eyes sparkled as though a beam of light
shone into the depths of her soul. The tiniest hint of a smile lifted
the corners of her thin, drooping lips as she raised herself off the
pillow slightly. It happened so quickly that seventeen-year-old
Margaret wondered if anyone else had noticed this truly mo-
mentous event.

Upon entering the familiar room, she had wanted to throw
open the curtains and raise the shades, but for some reason, they
were drawn, making the room seem dreary…to match the mood
of this morbid vigil, she supposed. Extra chairs brought into the
spacious bedroom accommodated her many paternal relatives
who either wept quietly or spoke in hushed tones. Margaret drew
comfort in the knowledge that all tears were genuine, and all
mourners were sincere in their grief. Her grandmother, she decided, knew how to die, just as she had known how to live…with
dignity, deep faith, and love borne of a pure heart.

Olivia Monroe was intimately acquainted with each person gathered that day. She accepted them—flaws and all—because she had nurtured each relationship throughout her purposeful life. She remained interested and interesting until that, her final, day. Margaret had never had to question her grandma's love because the woman had treated her with utmost respect from her earliest memory. She always felt more like her close friend than her grandchild.

When Margaret first approached the familiar four-poster bed (adorned with its creamy gauze canopy), tears streaming down her cheeks, her grandmother's only words were, "my Maggie," but those two simple words spoke volumes. This final, weak utterance prompted the happiest memories of Margaret's life, and unexpectedly, all of them washed over her like a powerful waterfall cascading off a mountain ledge. She had expected a cold, unfamiliar grasp. Instead, a warm, healing balm flowed through the tiny, bony hand into hers and permeated her whole being. That, she sensed, was her dear grandma's ultimate gift to her. That lesson on dying well was as precious as the many lessons on living that Olivia Monroe had imparted through the years. What a gentle teacher she had been, that strong, indomitable woman!

Margaret had never felt close to her maternal grandmother, even though they lived in the same town. The only quality required of a grandparent is unconditional love, and while she knew (on an intellectual level) that Grandma Stanford loved her, there always hung an unspoken cloud of disapproval. Grandma Stanford was deeply religious and highly moral. She wore her piety on her sleeve like a badge of honor. To her, religion consisted of multiple sets of rules. Margaret had felt that she never quite measured up to the expectations. She remembered feeling guilty when she couldn't grieve at Grandma Stanford's funeral. She had wanted to cry, but the tears wouldn't come.

"The poor child is in shock," she heard someone comment during the reception. "She hasn't shed a tear or eaten a thing all day."

The dishonesty of it all filled Margaret with guilt, but because grief was expected, she obliged with her best somber countenance until, finally, the long day ended. By the time the house was empty of mourners and well-wishers, she felt both exhausted and ravenous. Acting, she decided, was hard work. She had managed to act herself into a state of genuine depression that was difficult to shake. Upon later reflection, she supposed that professional actors must find it challenging to emerge from the characters they portrayed, especially sinister or gloomy characters. *Perhaps that accounts for the dramatic personal lives they often lead. They're always playing a part*, she conjectured. *Fantasy and reality probably become so intertwined that it's impossible to separate them.*

Chapter 6

Margaret and Sara reached the Intensive Care unit. Sara's mouth was moving, but once again, her friend's mind had drifted so that she caught only the end of the sentence. "…right here if you need me," Sara finished.

"Aren't you coming in?" Margaret asked, with panic returning unbidden like an annoying commercial that continually interrupts one's favorite television program.

"I can't," answered Sara. "They allow only one visitor at a time."

Margaret wanted to argue, but realized it would be a waste of energy. The same nurse whom Sara had met earlier approached, and Sara inquired, "Is there any change, Nurse?"

"She's getting weaker. Are you Margaret?" Margaret nodded in response to the question directed at her. "Please come in. She's been asking for you."

Why? Why me? Margaret wanted to scream, but all she could manage was a series of involuntary nods, like a doll whose head bobs up and down on the dashboard of a vintage car.

Noticing the color draining from Margaret's face, the kind nurse put her arm around the young woman's shoulders and gently, but firmly, led her into the imposing room.

Corinne looked surprisingly peaceful, and although her face was ashen and tubes protruded in all directions, she appeared quite lovely. Until this moment, Margaret had not thought of her as attractive, but with Corinne's normally severe ponytail released to frame her face, for the first time, she looked relaxed, even pretty.

"She has been unconscious most of the last hour," the nurse was saying. "Dr. Murphy expects her to slip into a coma any time."

"Can't he operate or something?" Margaret asked, still not able to comprehend the severity of Corinne's condition.

"I'm afraid not, dear. Her injuries are too severe. He can't understand what's keeping her alive. If only she had been wearing a seatbelt..."

"She wasn't wearing a seatbelt?" Margaret exclaimed, incredulous. Just then Corinne's eyes fluttered.

"Margaret?" Corinne whispered weakly; her voice was barely audible. She seemed so utterly vulnerable, so childlike, that Margaret rushed to her side. In an instant, all of the anger and resentment of the last year melted away. There lay a young woman, alone, afraid, and dying before her time. From the moment that she entered the room, Margaret was aware of negative energy in the air, and a general heaviness engulfed her. She felt deeply chilled, although the room was quite warm. She had only watched one other person die, but this, she sensed, would be a very different experience.

Corinne was becoming agitated. Margaret touched her shoulder gingerly.

"It's okay, Corinne. I'm here. You just rest. I'll be right here."

Corinne needed to speak, though. She desperately needed to tell Margaret something before it was too late. "Mother!" Corinne choked.

"No, Corinne. It's me, Margaret."

"Listen, please," uttered the dying woman weakly. She was heavily sedated, and her eyelids refused to stay open. Margaret drew closer in order to hear her faint voice over the beeping sounds produced by various monitors.

"Had to," Corinne breathed.

She's willing herself to stay awake, Margaret decided.

"Didn't mean to...kill..."

She's out of her head, was Margaret's next observation. She knew that no one else had died in the wreck.

"You didn't kill anyone, Corinne. No one died."

"Listen!" Corinne repeated huskily, this time jerking her hand on top of Margaret's hand. It was clammy and sent shivers through her entire arm. She wanted to pull away, but instead, she cradled Corinne's hand between hers. All feelings of malice toward her cantankerous co-worker began to fade as the gravity of this situation became more evident. Corinne was sleeping again. Margaret glanced up at the heart monitor and noticed that it registered 52 beats per minute. Then it would shoot up to 98 or 99 and back down to 50 or 52. She sat still for what seemed like hours, holding Corinne's hand. She could feel the erratic pulse in her wrist. Once, she thought Corinne's heart stopped beating, but the monitor was still beep, beep, beeping its gruesome duty.

Eventually, Margaret glanced at the window to the corridor where she hoped to see Sara. She wished Sara had been able to come in the room with her. If ever she needed a friend, the time was then. She would step outside just long enough to ask Sara for advice. *Will we be here all night?* she wondered. *Where is Corinne's family? Why has no one been located? Next of kin—isn't that what they're called?*

Margaret was praying for Corinne and for her own strength when a spasm shot through Corinne's arm, bringing Margaret back to attention.

"Accident," Corinne whispered. "Didn't mean to..."

"That's right, Corinne," responded Margaret. "It was an accident. It wasn't your fault."

"Go home!" Corinne gasped.

Margaret recoiled—shocked that Corinne would send her away after consistently summoning her, and only her, since arriving at the hospital. She tried to remove her hand, but the dying woman gripped it with surprising strength.

"Go home!" Corinne's eyes were wide and wild as she became more agitated. Margaret wondered if she should ring for a nurse, but now Corinne was clawing at her, pulling on her sleeve. "Mother!" Her final word was low and guttural, but uttered with such strength that Margaret felt terrified. It was as though some monstrous creature had entered Corinne's broken body. In one last surge of power, she sat up, jerking the IV tube out of her other arm. She let out a final, grotesque gasp that sounded like she had drowned in her own saliva…and then it was over.

Margaret tried to move—to call out—but her body felt frozen in place. That mere second or two before the nurses rushed into the room felt like an hour—an hour in which Margaret was completely alone in the world. She couldn't think, she couldn't speak, and she couldn't move. A nurse had to pry Corinne's stiff, but lifeless hand open to release her unwitting captive.

Amidst a flurry of activity, Sara, who had followed the nurses into the room, was helping Margaret to stand on wobbly legs and trying to lead her, gently, to the corridor where Jonathan was waiting.

Upon seeing Margaret's ashen face, Jonathan rushed forward to help Sara support her until they could get her to a chair. She couldn't seem to catch her breath or keep her legs under her. When the trio finally reached a row of chairs along the opposite wall, she was grateful to feel grounded.

"She's gone," Margaret whispered once she caught her breath. "She thought I was her mother."

A voice on the intercom paged Dr. Murphy, but before he arrived, an orderly was already pushing the crash cart out of Corinne's room, followed by two nurses. All the flurry of the past five minutes had come to a halt, and everyone seemed to be moving in slow motion. Margaret felt like she was awaking from a nightmare, but this was no dream.

Jonathan stood and approached one of the nurses. Margaret noticed her lips moving, but couldn't tell what she was saying. It didn't matter. She knew Corinne was dead. She—and only she— knew the exact moment at which Corinne's tortured soul left her body, filling the hospital room with polar air.

"The nurse said she went peacefully," Jonathan was reporting.

Oh, no she didn't! Margaret thought, shivering.

"She wants us to wait for Dr. Murphy," Jonathan continued. "He was in surgery when they paged him."

"We need to get Maggie out of here," Sara insisted. "She's a mess!" Turning to Margaret, she added, "You're coming home with me tonight."

Margaret didn't argue—didn't have the strength even if she had wanted to resist. This was one Friday night she would be grateful for company.

It didn't take long for Dr. Murphy to pronounce Corinne dead. It was merely a formality, anyway. It seemed to Margaret that the whole Intensive Care unit had grown silent. There were no windows nearby, and she wondered how dark it was outside the hospital. Without her wristwatch on, she had no idea of the time. Had a lifetime passed since she and Sara stepped off the elevator? Dr. Murphy finally came to speak to them. Before they could stand, he pulled a chair close to the trio and sat down. He looked very tired, Margaret observed. *This must be the most difficult part of an otherwise rewarding career*, she thought, fleetingly.

"I'm so sorry," he was saying. "There really wasn't anything we could do. Is there anyone we can notify? Her only personal effects were her driver's license and a credit card. Did she have any family in town?"

"She lived alone," remarked Jonathan. "I never heard her speak of any family."

"Me either," Sara agreed, shaking her head. "I never even knew where she lived."

"East Monument," the doctor interjected. "We tracked her address through the DMV. Her phone number is unlisted, but the police went to her house. They said no one answered the door." Then, turning to Jonathan, he added, "We thought maybe your Human Resources department could provide some information. We'll need to know what to do with the…" He hesitated, obviously trying to be sensitive to their feelings. "…her remains," he said quietly.

"I'll check into it first thing Monday morning," Jonathan offered.

"Good. Thank you. We'll keep her in our morgue until we hear from you."

"Let's get out of here," Sara said, feeling anxious to put the whole evening behind them. "Do you feel okay to walk, Maggie?"

"I'm fine." Margaret tried to sound convincing, but she still felt unsteady. She took a deep breath and stood, hoping her legs would support her. It didn't help that she had only had a glass of wine earlier and no dinner. With Sara at one elbow and Jonathan at the other, she managed to reach the elevator where they descended to the parking garage.

Sara's condo was only a few blocks from the hospital. In a matter of minutes, she had settled Margaret in her favorite leather recliner and covered her with the afghan that her parents had sent as a housewarming gift two years ago. Sparky, Sara's cocker spaniel, met them at the door, with tail wagging furiously. Although Margaret wasn't much of a pet person, she adored Sparky. A well-behaved dog, he never jumped on her and seemed to sense when she needed her space. He was resting beside her within reach of her dangling hand. Margaret felt comforted by Sparky's soft, curly fur, and as she repeatedly ran her fingers over the same spot on the dog's head, they both settled easily into the familiar routine of Margaret's frequent visits.

"How about a cup of tea?" Sara was asking as Margaret began to realize where she was and how she had gotten there.

"Thanks. That would be great. Do you have herbal?"

"Sure. Mandarin orange, I think. Have you had any dinner?"

"No, but I don't think I could eat anything."

"Let's start with the tea," her friend offered. "I'll bring some toast, and maybe you can take a few bites."

Margaret knew she couldn't possibly swallow anything solid, but without the strength to debate the issue, she allowed Sara to pamper her.

"Listen, I'm sorry to leave you alone, but poor Sparky hasn't been out all day." Sara was carefully handing Margaret a steaming cup of tea. "Here, sip on this and try to relax. We won't be long." As soon as Sara mentioned Sparky's name in connection with the word "out," her dog bolted to the door and was anxiously spinning in circles.

"Hold still, you crazy mutt! How do you expect me to…?" It was the same dance every evening: Sparky twisting in all directions and Sara struggling to fasten his leash to a gyrating collar. Ordinarily, Margaret would crack a joke about how Sara should trade him for a goldfish, but joking wasn't in her tonight. Sara just barely managed to grab an umbrella as Sparky dragged her out the door.

In the silence of the empty condo, Margaret was forced to relive the events of the evening. She wanted to cry, but couldn't summon the strength. Furthermore, she couldn't decide exactly *how* she was feeling, other than bone tired. Was it sadness or merely confusion? Her head was pounding, and she just wanted to forget everything that had happened—wanted to shake the awful foreboding and especially the feeling of Corinne's clammy death grip. A shiver shot through her despite the hot tea and cozy afghan.

Why did she think I was her mother? Sara, the nurses, and Jonathan all said Corinne was calling my name. Why would she ask for me and then send me away? Something didn't quite fit, but Margaret wanted to push it all out of her exhausted mind—just for tonight.

I won't miss Corinne, she confessed silently, *but I can't believe she's dead. I mean, I didn't want her to die. I certainly didn't want to watch her die! She seemed so alone—so tortured! I'll never be able to get that scene out of my mind. …Okay, okay, give it a rest, just for tonight. It's all too much to…* When Sara and Sparky returned only moments later, Margaret was asleep. The barely touched tea and toast lay on the end table beside her chair.

"Come on, Sparky," Sara whispered, "Let's get you some dinner." By this time, it was after 10:00 PM, and Sparky, who was accustomed to eating at six, gobbled his bowl of Purina nearly in one gulp and dutifully followed Sara to her bedroom, where he settled into his favorite spot at the foot of her brass bed.

Deciding to forego her usual shower, Sara quickly brushed her teeth and climbed into bed. She grabbed the remote control and set the timer to automatic shut-off even before selecting a channel. She didn't intend to watch anything but needed the noise to distract her from unbidden thoughts.

Chapter 7

It was surprising that Sara Bowman and Margaret Monroe had, so instantly, gravitated toward each other since they were worlds apart in…well, everything, really. Even in appearance, they were at opposite ends of the continuum: Sara was tall and slim, obviously Scandinavian in ancestry. Margaret was five-feet-three inches tall on a good day and had always had to watch her weight. Most days she cursed her naturally curly, brunette tresses, but Sara either ignored or countered her complaints since her own stringy blond hair caused her equal frustration.

Two years before, the two women had become friends almost instantly when they met in the Human Resources Department of Beeston Design Firm. Coincidently, they were applying for the same position, but in the end, Jonathan decided he needed both of them. Beeston had just accepted a mammoth contract with an international firm, and because the women represented diametrically opposing design perspectives, he decided they would complement each other.

Their homes reflected this juxtaposition. Sara's condominium was sleek and contemporary with a Danish influence. She knew how to make a sophisticated statement with brown. Her only reference to bygone eras was the brass bed from her childhood bedroom. It still had a dent where she and her sister Charley had fought over a game of Scrabble. Charley insisted that xanadu was not a legitimate word and accused Sara of cheating. A brawl ensued in which Scrabble tiles went flying about the room, and one wooden rack, grabbed furiously out of Sara's hand, struck the headboard with a thud. The girls understood (from previous rows) that their parents would not break up their fights, so the scuffles usually dissolved into tickling, giggling, and calling each other made-up names like "Buttella!" or "Uglinski!" This particular fight, however, ended abruptly when the sisters realized what had happened to their great-grandmother's antique brass bed. They never knew when their mother discovered the transgression. They spent the next ten guilt-ridden years piling pillows high enough to cover the damage (or so they thought).

"Your Aunt Martha and I slept in that bed, and your grandmother, before us," shared Sara's mother the day Sara moved out. "I want you to have it. Maybe you can get that dent in the headboard fixed before you pass it on to *your* first-born." Her all-knowing, nonjudgmental smile had given Sara strength and courage more than once in her eighteen years of life. At the time, Sara could not have anticipated how often she would long for her mother's special brand of unconditional love in the years to come, as she passed into adulthood.

Four years later (after the news that Charley had been wounded in the Gulf War), Sara spent many sleepless nights caressing the cool brass of her antique headboard, worrying, wondering, and remembering: the fun, the fights, but most of all, the friendship between sisters. Charley returned from the Gulf just before Sara's college graduation. Her wound eventually healed, but she was a different person, somehow. Gone was the spunky little girl who teased, annoyed, and worshiped her older sister. Sara tried to encourage Charley to talk about her experiences—they had always shared everything—but Charley would quickly avert her eyes or walk away from all inquiries. "It's over now," was all she would say.

One day, Sara determined, *Charley will come for a visit and share our childhood bed. One day, when the timing is perfect, she'll spill her guts to her big sister and let the real healing begin.*

Margaret's house was the exact antithesis of Sara's condominium. Antique furniture surrounded her, and she selected delicate floral patterns in a muted color palette. She loved her colonial with the white shutters and big front porch. She fell in love with her house the instant she saw it. It was almost as if she had first seen it in her dreams. It reminded her of Judge Hardy's home in those old Andy Hardy movies that she and her father enjoyed watching together. After her father's knee surgery, they had spent two entire days watching an Andy Hardy marathon on the classic movie channel. For two glorious days, she sat spellbound, getting up only to wait on her father or attend to various calls of nature. Her excuse, of course, was that Dad needed her, but truthfully, she just could not get enough of that house: the columned front porch, white picket fence, high ceilings, superb crown molding, and perfectly draped tall windows. She imagined that, if she could live in that magical house, life would be perfect. Judge Hardy's house remained her standard even through design school. She enjoyed learning as much as possible about every architectural style and decorating technique, but one day, she would live in a house like the Hardy family from Carvel, Idaho. It didn't matter that no such house actually existed.

Chapter 8

Corinne Melton had never shared any aspects of her personal life with her co-workers—not that anyone really cared to know more about her. Mostly, they avoided her (which wasn't difficult since she ate lunch in her office with the door closed and left precisely at 4:00 PM every day). She didn't seem shy. Rather, she exuded lack of interest in forging relationships. Was she simply antisocial or could she be hiding something? Every few weeks Sara and Margaret would resolve, again, to be nice to her—to give her one more chance, but Corinne would either ignore them or create conflict in some way. Just this week, Margaret had asked Corinne when she thought the samples would arrive for the Redmond contract. Jonathan had assigned Margaret all of the interior finishes on the project, and Corinne was responsible for fabric selections.

Jonathan preferred to have his staff collaborate on projects, capitalizing on each designer's strength. Margaret enjoyed sharing and comparing ideas. Whenever she and Sara worked together, there was a sense of mutual respect. Neither felt threatened by the other's suggestions. It was different with Corinne. She seemed to perceive suggestion as criticism and would begin immediately (and aggressively) to defend her position. Often it was impossible to follow her line of reasoning because she seemed to contradict herself. Most annoying was the way she cleaned up her act whenever Jonathan came within earshot. As far as Jonathan was aware, all members of his team worked well together. On a regular basis, however, Margaret and Sara would take turns complaining about Corinne's attitude.

"Now what?" was all that either would have to ask whenever met with *the look*. Heated words would spill out (in hushed tones) behind the closed door of one office or the other until the anger diffused and work could resume.

"Am I imagining it, or did Corinne just lie to Jonathan about why she missed the deadline on the Redmond project?" Margaret had spouted just a day ago. "She made it sound like it was my fault, but I know when she placed that fabric order. There's no way the custom upholstery could have been completed on time! How dare she insinuate that I failed to meet with the client on schedule! I had already met with Mrs. Redmond twice before she left for the Bahamas. I even invited Corinne to the meetings, but she claimed to have an 'unavoidable conflict' each time!"

"Yeah, I remember," confirmed Sara. "She left work early three days in a row last week, citing 'personal reasons.'"

"I didn't think she *had* a personal life," observed Margaret, instantly feeling snide. "Come to think of it, we still don't know anything about her. She never mentions a family, and she doesn't seem to have any friends."

"With that attitude, she couldn't possibly have friends!" Sara agreed. "All we really know is that she rides the bus to work most days, brings her lunch every day, and eats alone at her desk so she can leave an hour early."

"For all we know, she could have a criminal record. She could be using an alias, or maybe she's in the witness protection program!" Margaret was raving, but Sara had learned just to listen, allowing her friend to work through her outrage. Margaret had done the same for her many times.

Finally calmer, Margaret announced that the next day she would confront Corinne about the lie. "I will not let her jeopardize my reputation with Jonathan!"

The promised confrontation consisted of Corinne playing the role of victim and, somehow, managing to leave Margaret feeling guilty. It turned out to be Corinne's last week at Beeston Design Firm.

Chapter 9

Sara drifted back to sleep sometime before the TV shut off. At 6:05 AM, she heard sounds coming from her kitchen. The smell of freshly brewed coffee wafting through the condominium grabbed her attention. She wondered how long Maggie had been up and whether she had slept soundly. The events of the previous evening came rushing back, unbidden, like a strange nightmare. Was Corinne really dead, or had she dreamed it?

Sparky had already jumped off the bed and was waiting patiently for his sleepy-eyed mistress to open the bedroom door. "Hey, houseguest! Don't you know it's Saturday morning?" she asked, trying to persuade her heavy legs to carry her in the direction of the coffee pot. She felt like she hadn't slept at all.

"I'm sorry I woke you," Margaret responded. "I just couldn't sleep any longer."

"I should have made up the sofa bed for you, but I couldn't bear to wake you last night. You were wiped!"

Maggie was sprawled on the sleek sofa, with feet propped on the glass coffee table, sipping a mug of fresh coffee. "Listen, thanks for letting me crash here. I really didn't relish going home to an empty house after…" At that moment, the phone rang.

"Who in the world would call me at 6 AM on Saturday?" Sara glanced at the caller ID and recognized the number. "It's Jonathan," she announced, with surprise filling her voice. "Jonathan, what's up?"

"I'm sorry to call so early, Sara, but I thought you and Margaret would want to know."

"Know what?"

"Corinne's mother was found dead last night."

Sara stopped pouring her coffee mid-stream and set the pot down hard on the granite counter, nearly shattering it.

Margaret had started toward the kitchen as soon as Sara announced the caller, taking care not to spill coffee on the plush white carpet. With the condo's open floor plan, she could have heard Sara's end of the conversation from the living room, but her friend's startled reaction warranted closer inspection.

"What? What did he say?" she urged. Sara's hand shot up as if to signal, "Wait a second."

Sara, turning her attention back to the phone conversation, was grilling Jonathan. "Corinne's mother? You mean, she *did* have a family?" (There was a pause.) "Right here in town? Holy Cow!" (There was another pause.) "Murder? Holy Cow!"

"What is it?" Margaret interjected. "Put him on speaker!"

"Hold on, Jonathan. Let me put you on speaker so Maggie can hear. Now start at the beginning."

"Something doesn't add up," observed Margaret later in response to Jonathan's recount of the police report.

"Do you think Corinne killed her mother?" asked Sara. "She was unpleasant and weird, but was she actually capable of murder?"

The two friends were eating bagels and cream cheese at Sara's bistro table. Sparky lay at their feet, waiting for any sign of attention. It was a picture-perfect spring morning. Billowy clouds suspended from a bright blue sky, and a gentle breeze carried the smell of bacon from a nearby apartment. The outside temperature wasn't yet warm enough to use her balcony. Sara had placed the breakfast table just inside the sliding glass doors for the winter. Her balcony overlooked a well-manicured park with a duck pond in the center. Nearby was a playground where the voices of children resonated on Saturday mornings. They would appear soon, she anticipated, with their tricycles or skateboards.

Sara thought the sound of laughing, squealing children represented all that was good in the world. She hoped that, some day, she would have children—at least two. They would go to the park every Saturday morning to run, play, and grow in the sunshine. She hoped Alan wanted children as much as she did, and suddenly realized they hadn't discussed this very important topic yet. First, she must make sure Alan felt as committed to the relationship as she did. He was different from the other men she had dated. He seemed stable and, well, ordinary…the kind of man whom one doesn't notice immediately, but who, upon examination, would make a good husband and father.

"I wonder why Corinne never mentioned her mother," Margaret was saying. "She never mentioned any family, for that matter." Suddenly she was standing, like a soldier snapping at attention. "Sara, I have to get into that house!" Her eyes were darting here and there. Sara knew that look. It meant that Maggie's mind was working overtime. Nervous energy filled her friend, creating jerky motions as she began to clear the table. Startled by the sudden movement, Sparky moved to a safer location in the living room.

"Leave that. I'll get it," offered Sara, but Maggie had already forgotten her intended task and was gathering up her raincoat and purse.

"What are you saying, Maggie? You can't cross a police line. You know the house will be under surveillance!"

"Listen, Sara," Margaret continued, not even hearing her friend's warning, "I need a shower and some fresh clothes. I'll be back in an hour to pick you up."

"Wait!" Sara called as Margaret started for the door.

"This can't wait, Sara. There might be evidence that will get disturbed if we wait."

"Well, first of all, you may recall that you don't have a car, and secondly…"

"Oh yeah, that's right," Maggie interrupted. "Okay, Plan B." By this time, Margaret was a bundle of caffeine-laced adrenalin. "I'll wait while you get dressed. Then you can drive us to my house and…"

"Did it ever occur to you that I might have plans today? And, besides, I don't relish the idea of breaking and entering."

"What plans? Alan's on a business trip and…"

"Okay. Okay, so I don't have plans, but I also don't fancy jail time! I really don't want to get involved, Maggie!"

"Come on, Sara. We're already involved, and you know it."

"I can't believe I'm letting you talk me into this," Sara finally spouted with resignation, as she headed for the shower. "This is crazy! Hey, take Sparky out, will you? Who knows how long we'll be in the slammer?"

"Quit whining and hurry! Come on, Sparky. Let's go find a tree, and no dawdling!"

Chapter 10

Little more than an hour later, with the help of Margaret's GPS, the two conspirators managed to locate Monument Avenue. "What did Jonathan say the address was?" inquired Margaret.

"220...we're in the 400 block," reported Sara.

"Okay, let's park a block away and walk. That way my car won't be spotted near the crime scene," Maggie responded, noticing that she was sounding more and more like Nancy Drew.

"Wow, look at these amazing, old Victorians!" Sara remarked, adding, "Too bad they're so run down. I'll bet this was some ritzy neighborhood in its heyday."

"How sad that it hasn't been maintained," Margaret added. "That beautiful wrap-around porch is about to fall off," she observed, pointing to one of many ramshackle dwellings that lined the street. She turned onto a side street and found a place to park.

As they rounded the corner on foot, they continued to notice one dilapidated house after another with layer upon layer of peeling paint, as well as unkempt yards made worse by discarded rusty lawn furniture or trash. The few remaining piles of snow were brown, and the old, leafless trees seemed sad and tired. The sidewalks buckled in places, so the women had to step gingerly to keep from tripping.

"This neighborhood is stuck in the Depression," Sara observed.

"It *is* depressing!" Margaret added.

In a matter of minutes, they were facing house number 220. "This can't be it!" they both remarked at the same time. "Holy Cow!" exclaimed Sara. "Corinne lived here?"

The three-story Victorian was set close to the street. Peeling green paint exposed naked clapboards to the elements. Some of the windows were covered with boards, and several shutters hung loosely. Yellow crime scene tape surrounded the tiny front yard, but there were no other signs of police presence in the vicinity. In fact, there seemed to be no signs of life anywhere on the street. It felt eerie, like the opening scene of an Alfred Hitchcock movie.

"This house has to be haunted," Sara observed, shivering.

"Come on! Let's see if we can get in." Margaret was already moving toward the back yard.

"You can't be serious, Maggie!"

"Of course, I'm serious." At that moment, she noticed movement from the house next door. Someone had been watching them, but quickly retreated behind closed draperies as soon as Margaret turned in the direction of the window.

"Somebody saw us," she announced, grabbing Sara's arm. "Come on. We'll go around the other way."

"How many years do accomplices serve?" Sara asked, as she reluctantly followed her bossy friend to the west side of the house. They carefully lifted the yellow tape, each allowing the other to pass under the ineffective barrier. At the rear of the overgrown gravel driveway stood a one-car, detached garage. Margaret surmised that, most likely, it once served as a carriage house. On this side, they found a ground floor window located between the garage and house. Here, the out-building would prevent further scrutiny from nosy neighbors. She wondered if this window might allow them access to the house.

"Find something I can stand on," she directed. "I can't quite reach it." Sara, who now resigned to her role as aider and abettor, looked around, finally noticing an old abandoned tire propped against the back of the garage. "How about this?" she offered.

"That'll do for starters. How about that tub? Do you think it's wide enough to stack on top of the tire?" The tub was actually a discarded wooden barrel that looked like it had once served as a flowerpot. The partners in crime managed to roll it to the tire they had placed under the window and tip it upside down.

"Make sure nobody's watching," Margaret was still issuing orders, trying to keep her reluctant accomplice on task. "Now, help me up and steady the barrel." From her precarious perch, she was able to reach the window. She could see that the lock was missing, but declared the window "impossible to budge."

"Let me try," offered Sara. "If we can just get it started, maybe we can wedge something through the opening. See what you can find." Margaret climbed down and began searching the overgrown yard for something to use as a lever. Just then, they heard voices. "Get down," Margaret whispered. "Somebody's coming."

Reflected in the windows of adjacent houses, they could see flashing blue lights. "Holy Cow, Maggie! It's the cops! Now what?"

"We have to get out of here! Help me move this stuff out of sight."

With surprising strength, each woman grabbed an object of incrimination and half-rolled, half-dragged it behind the garage. They could hear voices and a police radio coming from the street.

As Margaret glanced around frantically, she noticed a narrow alleyway between the property lines of adjacent houses. It offered just enough space to accommodate a storm gutter, but hastily, she decided it was their only means of escape.

"Come on," she ordered, grabbing her friend's sleeve. "This way!" Single file, they squeezed sideways along the fence line, finally emerging on the next street.

"That was close!" Sara puffed, out of breath more from excitement than exertion. "Let's get out of here!"

"We can take this back street to my car," Margaret observed. "Try to look casual." They resisted the urge to run, trying to appear that they were out for a Saturday morning stroll. After what seemed an eternity, they arrived at Margaret's car and climbed in, simultaneously sighing with relief like a well-rehearsed duet.

"We'll have to come back after dark," concluded Margaret.

"Are you crazy?" Sara shot back. "That nosy neighbor probably described us to the police, and they'll be waiting for us."

"Don't be silly, Sara! We'll ditch these clothes and tuck our hair under hats. No one will be the wiser."

"Forget it! That house is spooky enough in the daytime, and besides Alan's coming back tonight. Why is this so important to you, anyway? What do you think you're going to find?"

"I don't think Corinne murdered her mother. She was trying to tell me something before she died."

"She's gone now, Maggie. It's over!"

"No, it isn't. I think Corinne was asking me to help her."

"You said she thought you were her mother."

"That's what I thought at first, but suppose she was asking me to *go* to her mother? Maybe I misunderstood. Maybe we've all misunderstood Corinne. You should have seen her, Sara—so tormented! It may be too late to befriend her, but I have to find out who she really was."

Chapter 11

Margaret awoke from a disturbing nightmare, but couldn't quite recall the details. Someone or something was chasing her through the halls of a large, dimly lit house, or maybe it was her old high school building. All she could recall clearly was that her legs felt leaden and would only move in slow motion. Along the corridor, she found every door locked. There was no escape! She felt relieved to wake up, but couldn't shake the feeling of doom left by the dream.

Sara had invited her to spend the night again, but Margaret assured her she would be fine alone. "Anyway, Alan won't relish having 'ol' Mags' underfoot on his first night back," she reminded Sara.

"Okay, but call if you need me. Alan will be jetlagged, anyway, and we'll probably just spend a quiet day at home tomorrow. Hey, you're not planning to go back to that house, are you? It's just too creepy!"

"Not without my accomplice," Margaret assured her.

"You promise?"

"Of course!" Margaret really intended to keep her promise.

Chapter 12

Sunday dawned bright and sunny. When Margaret stepped onto her front porch to retrieve the newspaper, she noticed that the sky was clear and the trees displayed visible buds. The forsythia bush at the corner of her lot was beginning to bloom, and her tulips and daffodils would soon follow. She eagerly awaited the explosion of color from hundreds of bulbs that she so liberally buried each fall. She could hardly wait to start cleaning out the flowerbeds, planting new perennials, and filling in with colorful annuals. Gardening was one of her most satisfying pastimes. She had created so many flower beds that scarcely any grassy areas remained in her yard. As soon as the last piles of snow melted, she would begin the arduous, but gratifying, task of preparing the soil and applying fresh mulch.

It was still too chilly to sit on the porch swing and read the newspaper, but the crisp morning air filled her with anticipation of that first warm Sabbath. For a few more weeks, she would take her newspaper and her coffee to the sunroom inside.

Bending down to retrieve what appeared to be little more than a bundle of advertisements, Margaret was taken aback by the front-page headline: "Local Woman Found Shot. Deceased Daughter Suspected of Murder." Ignoring the chill in the air, Margaret sank to the stoop and began to read:

The body of 62-year-old Agatha Melton was discovered Friday night in her home on Monument Avenue. Police say a neighbor called them after hearing screams and a single gunshot. Witnesses claim to have seen Melton's daughter, Corinne Melton, fleeing the scene. In a bizarre twist, the younger Melton died later that evening from injuries sustained in an automobile accident. Police are investigating the deaths of both women as possible homicides. Police spokesperson, Aaron Griffith, dubbed this case the strangest his department has ever handled. "There are many unanswered questions. Our department is not accustomed to dealing with such heinous crimes," Griffith stated.

Margaret never made it to her sunroom. Tossing the newspaper on the dining room table, she vaulted up the stairs to get dressed. "I have to get in that house! I have to find out what really happened!"

Normally, Margaret would spend a leisurely hour reading the Sunday paper and drinking at least two cups of coffee. Then she would prepare to walk the three blocks to church—a stunning cathedral she had discovered shortly after moving into the neighborhood. Although her parents raised her in the Baptist tradition, she longed for a more formal, liturgical worship service. Not only did St. John's Episcopal address her ceremonial longings, but also the grand architecture and magnificent pipe organ inspired her. The entire encounter left her feeling uplifted and somehow closer to God. One day she might become more involved, get to know the parishioners, and maybe even join the parish, but, for now, she preferred to remain an anonymous worshiper. On this day, Margaret had planned to pray for Corinne's soul, but suddenly, attending church was no longer on her agenda. A more urgent mission summoned her.

Margaret showered quickly, donned her favorite blue sweats, and pulled her shoulder-length curls back in a ponytail. Ordinarily, she wouldn't leave the house without applying make-up, but today there was only time for a touch of lip gloss. She and Sara had planned to return to the abandoned Victorian after dark the next day, when the neighbors wouldn't be as likely to notice them, but Margaret felt strangely compelled to proceed without delay. It was almost as if Corinne, herself, was drawing Margaret to the house. How would she gain entry without Sara to steady the makeshift ladder?

That's it, she realized. "I'll take a ladder...and a flashlight. With those heavy draperies drawn, it's likely to be dark inside even during the day, and I certainly don't want to draw attention by turning on lights...and gloves—I'll need gloves. Even though the police have probably finished their investigation, I don't want to take the chance of leaving fingerprints." She realized she was talking aloud again, a habit that grew more frequent lately. *I'm turning into an old, dotty spinster. Maybe I could have my own TV show,* The Spinster Sleuth.

Margaret had just squeezed a stepladder into the back seat of her blue Civic. It was a tight fit, but by positioning it diagonally, she managed to cram it in and shut the door. The ladder had been one of her first purchases after buying the house. She was determined to paint every room before moving day, and with Sara's help, she had succeeded. She chose cool colors—muted greens and blues—that reminded her of a fresh ocean view. The glossy, white molding represented clouds, she decided. Except for a few carefully chosen paintings and family photographs, she would keep the walls unadorned. She had inherited her grandmother's Persian rugs and could hardly wait to take them out of storage. First, she would have the worn walnut floors refinished, though.

She wanted her home to feel cozy, yet bright and cheerful. The sunroom was her favorite spot. It had become her sanctuary. Originally a screened porch, it had been converted by the previous owners into what the real estate brochure called a "Florida room." Somehow, the term didn't seem accurate—maybe because her only two visits to Florida conjured up memories of oppressive heat and humidity, senior living trailer parks, and pink flamingo lawn ornaments. She preferred to call it her "morning room" instead.

Margaret's morning room, situated on the back of the house, faced east. There it caught each day's first precious rays of sunlight. She filled it with palm trees, pink and purple bougainvillea, and lush hanging ferns. Her favorite books were there, displayed on a rattan bookcase that she had purchased at a yard sale. The newer rattan furniture with its comfortable cushions and colorful pillows invited one to settle in and spend the day. One oversized chair instantly became her special relaxing spot. She called it her "Vitamin D" chair. It was where she enjoyed her second cup of coffee after an early-morning run. It was where she meditated and read. She was determined to keep this a television-free zone. Her morning room would remain devoid of media to eliminate distractions. Only favorite books were allowed occupancy here, along with an array of tropical plants, of course.

She had fallen in love with an ornate, wooden birdcage during one of her many antiquing trips. She spent far too much of her meager salary on it, but every time she looked at it, she had to admit it was the perfect accent to this inviting oasis.

In her New York apartment, she had used a small breakfast nook for the same purpose. Ned preferred to hang out in her den, claiming that the furniture was more comfortable, but Margaret soon ascertained that the TV was what lured him there. At first, she thought she had much in common with Ned. He was a real estate agent, and she was addicted to open houses. They met at a home show shortly after Margaret moved to the city. She was renting an apartment with the intention of finding a house in Jersey as soon as possible, but it had to be just the right house. Her trip to the home show was partly for a work project and partly to confirm what she thought characterized her style. She wanted to ensure that her first house accurately represented her personality and taste. Someday, she might have to compromise, but this first home would be hers alone.

At the paint display adjacent to the Forrest Realty booth, Margaret was lost in her copious note-taking when she heard a male voice remark, "There's a woman who knows what she wants." Wondering if the man's words were directed at her, she swung around, nearly knocking over a carefully erected pyramid of paint cans.

"Excuse me?" she responded upon realizing she was the only woman in the immediate vicinity.

"You seem hell-bent on a mission," he continued, with blue eyes twinkling.

"Oh, yeah, I guess I'm a little intense. I only have one day to spend here, and I have to make a lot of decisions," she responded, not sure why she felt compelled to explain anything to this stranger. Maybe it had something to do with the fact that the stranger was a drop-dead Adonis. At this point, she couldn't remember whether Adonis had been blond or dark-haired, but it didn't matter. In her mind, this man epitomized what the handsome youth of Greek mythology surely must have looked like: thick blond, wavy hair; tall with an athletic build; and those eyes! She hoped she wasn't drooling.

"Hi, I'm Ned." He was holding out his hand. Suddenly, Margaret felt like a giddy schoolchild and hoped this handsome stranger didn't notice her shaking hand.

"Margaret," she offered. She wished she had styled her hair that morning instead of pulling it back in a ponytail and casually licked her lips to check for lip gloss. Well, at least she tried to act casual.

"So, are you building or renovating?" he asked. There was a friendly, confident manner about him (perfect qualities for a realtor, she observed).

"Actually, I'm working. I work for a design firm."

"Oh, so I guess you don't need the services of a realtor." She knew he was flirting, and she liked it.

"In fact, I do," responded Margaret, trying not to sound too eager. "I'm also hoping to buy a house soon." Just then, a customer (whom Ned had been helping before he spotted Margaret) demanded his attention. The woman was leafing through a property catalog at the opposite end of the counter.

"Yes, Ma'am. I'll be right there," he called. "Say, uh, Margaret?"

Is he a little nervous or did he forget my name already?

"Sir!" The customer was visibly irritated. Ned started in her direction, but not without making it clear that he intended to ensure future contact with Margaret.

"There's a great hotdog stand in front of the next tent. How about meeting me there at noon? We can discuss your options— for houses, I mean—and I'll even spring for lunch."

Later, as the new acquaintances ate hotdogs and drank lemonade in the warm summer sun, Margaret decided she had found the man of her dreams.

Chapter 13

Margaret had just shifted her transmission into reverse and was about to back out of the driveway when some idiot pulled in behind her, blocking her exit. "What the…?" she exclaimed, un-hooking her seatbelt and jumping out at nearly the same instant. "That's a good way to lose a headlight, Mister!" she shouted through his windshield.

"Sorry I startled you," the man responded as he stepped out of his car. "I didn't see your back-up lights until it was too late. Are you Margaret Monroe?"

"Yes, but as you can see, I was just leaving for an appointment."

"On Sunday?"

"Some people go to church on Sunday," she defended.

"You don't look like you're dressed for church." Who was this man and why was he challenging her?

"I'm Detective Dennison of Homicide, and I'd like to ask you a couple of questions. I promise not to keep you long."

It occurred to Margaret that Sara would say, "Holy Cow!" at a time like this. Someone at the crime scene must have identified her. At the time, she and Sara felt confident they had gotten away clean, but that curious neighbor must have turned them in. *How did he trace me to this address, and how did he learn my name?* she wondered. *Maybe Sara wasn't being hysterical after all. Maybe we are facing jail time!*

"Listen, Officer, Detective, or whatever, we were only…"

"Ms. Monroe," he interrupted, "I understand you were the last person to see Corinne Melton alive. I'm investigating the death of her mother."

Whew! she almost said aloud, hoping he hadn't noticed her sigh of relief.

"Would you mind answering a few questions?"

"I guess not," Margaret responded, relaxing a bit. "In fact, I'd be interested in learning what the police know about the case. What evidence do you have to implicate Corinne?"

"Witnesses saw her leaving the scene right after the shot was heard."

"Isn't it possible that she was running from the killer or maybe even going for help?"

"Wait. I thought the detective was supposed to ask the questions."

"Oh, sorry. But, you see, I don't believe Corinne murdered her mother."

"What makes you say that?"

"When she was in the hospital, she kept saying, 'It was an accident.' At first I thought she was talking about the car accident, but that was before I knew about her mother's death."

"How well did you know Ms. Melton?"

"We worked together, but nobody really knew her. We didn't even know she lived with her mother. She was very private."

"Why did she call for you when she was dying?"

"I have no idea. It's a complete mystery. We certainly weren't close."

"Did she ever speak of her mother?"

"Never. Not until that day. She was hallucinating, and she thought *I* was her mother. What about the weapon? Were there any fingerprints? Whose gun was it, anyway?"

"It was registered to Robert Melton, Ms. Melton's father who has been dead for nearly ten years."

"Say, Detective…"

"Call me Jeff."

"Okay, Jeff, do you suppose I could take a look inside Corinne's house?"

"Why? What would you be looking for?"

"I'm not sure—maybe nothing."

"We did a thorough search, Ms. Monroe."

"Margaret."

"Margaret, we gathered all the evidence that was available."

"In that case, I wouldn't be disturbing anything, would I, Detec...I mean, Jeff?"

Because of the bright morning sun, Margaret hadn't gotten a good look at the detective, but as he shifted positions, his form became shaded by the row of tall evergreens that bordered her driveway. The man's face was pleasant enough, she decided, but he needed a shave. Maybe he thought that dark, scruffy stubble was sexy, but she didn't. She had always preferred the clean-shaven look. She estimated his age to be mid-thirties and observed that he wasn't wearing a wedding ring. He had nice hands—not too smooth, but not rugged and work-stained like her father's hands had always been. She surprised herself by wondering how it might feel to hold hands with him.

"I'll see if I can get the key again. Since the captain thinks you and Ms. Melton were friends, maybe I can get you in to choose her burial clothes." His words made her shudder.

"You still haven't located any other family?" She queried.

"No, as I said, her father died some time ago, and no one else has come forward. What time do you get off work tomorrow?"

"Five o'clock, but I can leave early. I just finished a big contract, and I have some comp time coming." She wasn't sure why she added that last part, but for some reason, she felt compelled to share more about herself than was required. "Would it be all right if my friend, Sara, came along? She worked with Corinne, too, and was at the hospital when she died."

"Sure, I guess so, but I still don't see what you think you're going to find. Why don't I pick you up here at 4:00?" he suggested with a shrug of resignation.

"We'll be ready. Thanks."

As he turned to leave, Margaret found herself checking out his backside with approval, but quickly turned her attention to locating her cell phone. She sat in the car long enough to call Sara with the news and then decided it was a perfect day to walk to church, after all.

Chapter 14

Margaret really had tried to make the relationship with Ned work. He certainly wanted it to work, but on *his* terms. They spent every spare minute together, doing what *he* wanted to do. Every restaurant was *his* choice. While they shared a few common interests like running, open houses, and fine dining, Ned didn't seem interested in getting to know her better. In fact, he didn't seem to value who she was as a person. There were subtle put-downs that she ignored because she was in love. Most conversations remained surface chitchat, and the time they spent alone together, they spent in front of the TV. An avid sports fan, Ned seemed to schedule his life around televised athletic events.

After seven months of dating, Margaret was beginning to lose her sense of self in the relationship. She felt smothered and socially isolated. There was a definite physical attraction, but long ago, she had determined that it was essential to build an emotional and spiritual relationship devoid of sex, in order to find one's life partner. Ned never gave up trying to change her mind on that issue, but in the end, he would acquiesce reluctantly. He asked her to marry him weekly, but she put him off, saying she needed more time. Finally, one evening, as they were watching the Giants and the Cowboys—rather, she was reading as he watched the game—she came to a decision. She took a good, hard look at Ned.

This man doesn't have a clue about how to nurture a relationship. I can't imagine spending our next fifty years together like this, she concluded. *After acting just charming enough to attract my attention, now that we're a couple, he seems content to merely breathe the same air. I need more. I need someone with whom to share my thoughts and feelings and who shares his with me. It's not fair to continue stringing him along.* She decided she would break the news on their picnic scheduled for the next day in Central Park.

Margaret didn't sleep well that night. She agonized over how she would tell him. She really didn't want to hurt Ned. In a way, she did love him, but deep down, she knew they would eventually grow apart. It was better to end it right away than to marry and regret it later.

She had rehearsed and rehearsed her speech. She wanted to be sure that Ned understood how much she cared for him and that she wished only the best for him; however, a breakup is a breakup, and there's no easy way to accomplish it.

Ned hadn't seen it coming, hadn't suspected a thing, and reacted with shock. Next, he launched into an angry outburst, so verbally violent that joggers actually stopped to see what was causing all the commotion. *Why is it that men have to cover their true feelings with anger? Why can't they just act hurt, disappointed, or sad?* she wondered later, recalling the awkward scene. *Perhaps it makes them feel weak or even effeminate,* she finally determined. *American culture has really done a number on men!* She made a mental note to teach any future sons of hers how to handle their emotions in a healthy way.

In the end, Ned's extreme reaction confirmed what she had been sensing for a while. *He keeps his feelings so repressed that, when they finally rise to the surface, he reacts in the extreme. If we hadn't been in a public setting, I think he might actually have hit me. I certainly don't want to spend the rest of my life wondering what words or events might trigger the next explosion!*

The following day, she gave her notice at work and broke her apartment lease. She hadn't seen or heard from Ned Romney since, and she intended to keep it that way.

Chapter 15

On Monday afternoon, Margaret and Sara were waiting on Margaret's front porch when Detective Dennison arrived. As he alit from his unmarked cruiser and walked around to open the door for them, Margaret noticed that he had shaved. *Much better*, she thought. As soon as he shut the door behind them, Sara looked at her friend as if to say, "You failed to mention he's a hunk." A quick elbow jab cautioned her not to voice her thoughts. Jeff took the driver's seat, and they were on their way back to 220 East Monument Avenue.

"So, Detective, what do the police know about the case?" Sara inquired.

"Well, there were no signs of forced entry. In fact, the front door was unlocked. Mrs. Melton was found on the floor of her bedroom where she had been shot in the head."

"What about suicide? Could she have killed herself?" Margaret interjected.

"It's possible, but there were signs of a struggle, and there appeared to be two sets of fingerprints on the weapon."

"Whose fingerprints?"

"We don't know yet."

"How well did the neighbors know Corinne?" Margaret asked.

"Not well at all. It seems that she and her mother kept to themselves. In fact, some didn't even realize Mrs. Melton was still living—said they hadn't seen any signs of her since her daughter moved in nearly a year ago. Well, here we are, ladies. I have to check in with the station. Here's the key. I'll be right behind you."

"It's such a mess," Sara remarked as they climbed the rickety front steps. I can't imagine what the inside must look like."

"We're about to find out." Margaret turned the key and slowly opened the door. Nothing could have prepared the two professional decorators for what awaited them. It looked more like a salvage yard than a home. On either side of the large, open foyer was a parlor. Every corner and every surface held an unfathomable array of items. There were books, magazines, papers, antique vases, sculptures, paintings, dishes, clocks, and music boxes, for starters. Sara and Margaret (who frequented antique shops) had never seen anything to compare with the volume of merchandise assembled here.

"Holy cow!" was Sara's predictable reaction.

"Incredible!" Margaret added. "I've never seen anything like this before, even at estate sales."

"What do you make of it, Maggie?" Sara asked.

Detective Dennison, who had entered behind the horrified pair, offered an explanation. "Evidently, Mrs. Melton was off her rocker. She was what's called a hoarder."

"You can say that again!" Sara concurred.

"What does it mean? What is all of this stuff?" Margaret wanted to know.

"That's what hoarders do. They collect as many possessions as they can and never throw anything out. It's an addiction—a compulsion they can't control."

"But Corinne was a neat freak," Sara commented. "How could she live like this?" It was a rhetorical question.

Heavy drapes covered the windows, making the rooms dark and dreary. What furniture they could see beneath the debris was obviously as old as the house itself. Bypassing the large winding staircase, the trio continued its tour of the ground floor, through a formal dining room with a cobweb-adorned crystal chandelier suspended from the ceiling and mahogany crown molding throughout. Beneath the chandelier stood a beautiful, but dust-laden Queen Anne dining table with eight matching chairs, each upholstered in silk brocade. The floor-to-ceiling windows were clad in worn burgundy velvet. Threads of gold ran through the heavy panels. How grand this room must have been once! At that time, however, it resembled little more than a repository for yet more castoffs. At this point, Margaret and Sara, though speechless, sensed what the other was thinking.

Beyond the dining room, there was a large, updated kitchen. Not that it could be called modern by any stretch of the imagination, but it certainly wasn't representative of the Victorian era. Compared to the crowded, dusty rooms they had just passed through, it was relatively clean, at least around the sink. With the exception of a small dinette set, however, collections of every sort adorned each surface. In one corner, next to the back door, Margaret espied what appeared to be every issue of National Geographic magazine ever published. In another corner stood a country-style hutch filled to the brim with Wedgewood china and Waterford crystal. Beside it stood a tower of dining chairs that clearly required re-caning before they could be of use to anyone.

The only other room at the rear of the house, other than a small mudroom (filled to the ceiling with fireplace wood), lay beyond a curtained doorway. It seemed to have been annexed mid-century, or possibly converted from a porch. Unlike the other rooms, this space looked somewhat inhabited. The furniture was old and worn, and evidently, the room served as the main living space. On a low credenza sat a small TV that faced a slipcovered sofa and matching chair. Worn beige carpet covered the floor, and plantation blinds concealed the windows. The only other items included a maple-colored laminate coffee table and matching end table with a brass lamp, as well as one floor lamp and a rocking chair. Built-in bookcases lined one wall. While they were bulging at the seams with worn, dusty books, this room seemed relatively devoid of clutter.

Margaret's throat felt dry as she found her voice. "May we see the upstairs?" she finally managed to ask.

"Sure," answered Jeff, "but there's a whole third floor that's shut off from the rest of the house. Most likely, it has been boarded up for many years."

They reached the top of the once-grand marble staircase. Predictably, the landing was as cluttered as the first floor rooms. Shorter staircases leading in opposite directions flanked the wide upstairs hallway. The flight to their left funneled to a long, dark corridor, and to the right, they could see the boarded-up entrance to which Jeff had referred.

"What's this way?" Sara inquired, as they headed down the cavernous hallway.

"There are two large bedrooms opposite each other," Jeff answered. "The one at the front of the house is where Mrs. Melton was killed. Before you go in, I should warn you there's quite a lot of blood on the rug."

"Okay, thanks for the warning," Margaret responded, with her hand already on the doorknob. She slowly turned the knob, noticing, with curiosity, that the lock was on the outside. Looking at Sara, she inquired, "Are you ready?"

"Nothing could be more shocking than what we've already seen," Sara assured her.

"Everything is just the way we found it," Jeff explained. "You'll notice definite signs of a struggle."

A crumpled, blood-soaked rag rug lay in the center of the room beside a huge four-poster bed with its intricately carved mahogany headboard. The bed was unmade, its coverings spilling onto the floor. A lamp from the nightstand was overturned, as was the bench from an adjacent dressing table. Surrounding the rug was the chalk outline of the deceased.

"I thought they only did that in the movies," Sara commented.

"It's pretty much standard procedure in homicide cases," Jeff explained.

As Sara and Margaret glanced about the disheveled room, nothing else seemed remarkable. There was additional evidence that Corinne's mother had been more than just a collector. Trunks and boxes of all shapes and sizes lined the walls. They were overflowing with clothing, papers, gift-wrapping supplies, and Christmas decorations…enough accumulation to represent several lifetimes. The most surprising discovery, however, awaited them across the hall.

Chapter 16

Corinne's departure was about to be announced. Traffic on the L.A. freeway that morning was horrendous, nearly causing her to miss the flight. She was shocked to see David waiting for her at the gate, holding a long-stemmed red rose. She thought she lied convincingly that it was over between them—that she had met someone else. It was the only way to keep him from following her. Relocating to the east coast would mean certain ruin of a career that David had worked tirelessly to establish. He adored his work at Paramount, and she knew he would eventually resent her for taking him away. Yes, a clean break was best.

They met by chance at UCLA, just days before they would have gone their separate ways forever. At the time, it seemed providential. David, a native of California, had taught at the film school for nine years, just waiting for his chance to secure a position in Hollywood. He had always planned to be a cinematographer, rather than a professor of cinematography, but until the previous week, he had given up hope. Corinne, having just earned her master's degree in interior design, planned to move back east. New York, Philadelphia, or even Chicago would bring her close enough to her hometown that she could make the trip home in just a few hours, if necessary. The next week, she would prepare her resume and send it to every major design firm in each city. Surely, a full scholarship to UCLA and a 3.9 grade-point average would be enough to land her a desirable job, even in a competitive market.

Corinne hadn't been looking for love. In fact, she had worked hard to avoid it for the past five years. She had career aspirations, and no man was going to prevent her fulfilling her dreams. David wasn't just any man, though. He was warm, interesting, intelligent, and witty. Although he was several years older than she was, they connected immediately. He could hold her attention longer than anyone she had ever met, and for some reason (strange though it seemed to her), David found her fascinating.

Corinne always thought of herself as plain—homely, even—but from that first meeting in the campus coffee shop, David saw something beautiful in her that had nothing to do with her appearance. He said she was the most creative person he had ever met and that her soul was "as deep as the ocean." They could talk for hours about art history, classic literature, architecture, cinematography, and philosophy, just for starters.

By the end of the summer, they were sharing David's Malibu beach house and making plans to share the rest of their lives. Each morning, they walked along the shore drinking coffee from insulated mugs, letting the icy surf wake them from the toes upward. Nearly every evening they reveled in glorious Pacific sunsets from David's terrace. Soon thoughts of moving back east caused Corinne great anguish, yet she was becoming increasingly concerned about her mother, whom she hadn't seen in three years. Each December, she tried to go home for Christmas, but her mother discouraged the trip, claiming it was too far and too expensive.

"You need to focus all of your time and energy on school right now," she would say. "There'll be plenty of time to spend with your old mother after graduation."

Lately, whenever she phoned home, there seemed to be a new clue that something wasn't quite right. Since her husband's death several years before, Agatha Melton had grown increasingly melancholy. Of course, grief was to be expected, but this was different, somehow. Corinne wondered if grief, coupled with loneliness, had evolved into major depression. Her mother seemed to forget things, to become confused easily, and even to sound childlike at times. Agatha Melton wasn't old enough to be senile. *Could she be manifesting the initial stage of Alzheimer's?* Corinne wondered.

At first, she tried to handle the situation at long distance, but during her five years away, much had changed. Recently, she learned that her mother's doctor retired, and evidently the neighborhood of Corinne's childhood no longer existed. Without anyone else with whom to share family burdens, it was even impossible to find someone who could check on Agatha from time to time. At first, she tried to convince her mother to sell the house that she could no longer maintain. Agatha wouldn't hear of it. "This is the only real home I've ever known," she would argue.

Finally, Corinne decided it was time to visit her mother and try to make sense of the woman's strange behavior. It would be a quick trip while David was filming on location. He wouldn't even have to know about it. She would be back in time to welcome him home.

What she found was shocking! It convinced her that Agatha Melton could no longer live alone. With no one else upon whom to rely, Corinne knew her fate was sealed. She would return to Malibu just long enough to collect her belongings. David, she was convinced, would understand the sense of obligation that motivated her. He would insist on pulling up roots, abandoning a job that he loved (that he had earned), and moving across the country to be with her. She loved him too much to let him sacrifice his whole future for her.

Waiting, nervously, at the departure gate, David knew that this would be his last chance to change her mind. He *knew* she loved him. He sensed that there was more to her story than the jilted lover routine she had attempted awkwardly to convey. She was hiding something, all right, but it wasn't another lover. He was sure of that.

"I have to go, David! Just let me go, okay?"

"How can you leave like this, Corinne?" He implored. "How can you just walk away?"

"Please…it's better this way." Abruptly, coldly, she pulled from his grasp and edged in front of a couple with two small children, thrusting her boarding pass at the attendant. She needed to be sure he couldn't follow her onto the jet way. Had she looked back at him, the tears welling in his eyes might have changed her mind. She couldn't take that chance. Her own tears didn't abate until she reached the layover at O'Hare. Dividing the trip into two legs would throw David off her trail, she hoped. She would never again take the chance of letting anyone get that close.

Chapter 17

Behind the heavy, solid door of the Melton home, Margaret and Sara discovered a room that stood in stark contrast to the rest of the house. It was pristine, devoid of clutter, and tastefully decorated. "Holy Cow!" Sara exclaimed. "Have we just passed into another dimension?"

"Was this Corinne's room?" inquired Margaret of Detective Dennison.

"So it seems," he responded.

The furnishings were simple but tasteful, and obviously chosen with care. A well-executed oil painting that hung above the headboard immediately drew the visitors' eyes upward. Like a museum spotlight, the afternoon sun highlighted the portrait of a middle-aged man.

"Could that be Corinne's father?" Sara inquired.

"Yes, he matches various family photographs that we found throughout the house," answered Jeff.

Perfectly positioned throw pillows adorned the head of a carefully dressed bed, and a matching coverlet, in measured folds, draped across the foot. The shiny walnut floor boasted a well-preserved oriental rug that Margaret estimated to be at least one hundred years old. No heavy, velvet draperies smothered these windows. With a decorator's touch, they had been adorned with inexpensive, but tasteful voile panels and matching valances. The walls wore cheerful, buttery yellow paint, a color lifted from the blue and yellow bedspread that completed the French provincial design. An exquisite Louis XIV writing desk stood between the stately windows, and a comfortable-looking chaise, upholstered in blue linen, invited one into the tranquil scene.

As Margaret and Sara slowly scanned the tastefully appointed, spotless boudoir, their jaws dropped in tandem. Both women realized they had to know more about their mystifying colleague. Who was Corinne, really? What motivated her odd, abrasive behavior? What was her relationship with her mother? Why had she returned to her dilapidated childhood home last year? What had she been hiding? There were so many unanswered questions.

"Detective, I mean, Jeff," Margaret began, noticing his strong jaw line and deep brown eyes for the first time. "Would it be alright if we took a closer look around? We'll be careful not to disturb anything."

"We've completed our investigation, and besides, the actual crime scene is across the hall. Take your time. I'm off duty now, anyway. I'll wait for you downstairs."

"Thank you," Margaret and Sara said at the same time. "We won't be long," added Margaret.

The detective started toward the door, but turned back to face the pair. "Before you leave, please remember the supposed reason for this visit."

"Oh, right," recalled Margaret. "We'll pick out something for Corinne's funeral."

"Fine. Thanks. I want to look around one more time, myself. Something about this case just seems off," Jeff said as he left the room.

"You can say that again!" exclaimed Sara. Then, turning to Margaret, she asked, "What do you think we're going to find, Maggie?"

"I don't know—maybe nothing—but I have to figure out what made Corinne tick. What was she hiding, Sara?"

"Well, that's pretty obvious, isn't it? She didn't want anybody to know she lived in this dump or that her mother was a nutcase."

"No, there's something else. I just have a feeling there was more to Corinne than the unpleasant, reclusive person she hid behind."

"Well, let's get our morbid assignment over with, and then we can search for some clues. One of these must be a closet," Sara observed, motioning toward two doors on the opposite side of the room.

"Okay, you try that one," Margaret suggested. "I'll see what's in here."

"This is a bathroom…nothing here," reported Sara. "Nice claw-footed tub, though."

"Here's the closet," Margaret commented. "Help me find something…appropriate."

"This is so odd! We hardly even knew Corinne, and now we're rummaging through her closet," observed Sara.

"I know," Margaret agreed, with melancholy creeping into her voice. "Who could have predicted, last week, that today we'd be picking out Corinne's burial clothes?"

"Let's get this over with. I'm getting the creeps!" declared Sara.

"What about this blue suit?" Margaret suggested, adding, "I think blue might have been her favorite color."

"Fine. What about shoes?" Sara was trying to speed up the process.

Margaret realized she didn't know if corpses wore shoes, but decided to select a pair just in case they might be needed. "Here, put this on the bed," Margaret directed, handing the suit to Sara. "I'll look for some shoes."

Margaret was on her hands and knees, searching through Corinne's limited, but neatly arranged collection of footwear. She stood to push the hanging clothes apart and let in more light when Sara heard her cry, "Sara, look at this!"

"What? It had better not be a mouse, or I'm leaving this minute!"

"Come here! Look!" Margaret called. "What do you make of this?" At the back of the shallow closet, she had discovered a framed door, through which only one small person could possibly pass on hands and knees.

"It probably goes to the storage space under the eaves. Most of these old houses had them," Sara confirmed, relieved.

"Yeah, but this one is locked. Why would a storage area be locked, especially since all of the valuables in this house are in plain sight?"

"Good point," agreed Sara. "Let's see if we can find the key. I'll look in the desk. You take the bureau drawers."

The amateur sleuths made an exhaustive search of Corinne's tidy room: in the bureau, in the desk, on the nightstand, under the bed, and behind cushions and pillows. They even went through the pockets of her clothing.

"Bummer!" Sara finally uttered with defeat.

"Look at this!" cried Margaret.

"Did you find the key?"

Margaret had been rummaging through a hump-back trunk positioned at the foot of Corinne's bed.

"No, but I found a very interesting photo. I think it might be Corinne's family. The man is the same one in the portrait over her bed."

Sara moved closer to get a better look. "Holy Cow! Either this is a double exposure or Corinne has a twin sister!"

"They certainly are identical, aren't they?" Margaret agreed. "I wonder where she is. We should tell Jeff. Maybe the police can locate her."

"She should be notified that both her mother and sister have died. See if you can find something with her name on it—maybe a letter or some kind of keepsake," Sara urged.

"Help me look. I see more pictures in this box. Here's one with just the two girls. They're younger, maybe six or seven." Again, it was impossible to tell which of the identical girls Corinne was. With arms wrapped around each other, their faces glowed with toothless smiles. They were standing on the front porch of this very house, wearing matching pinafores. Like the first photograph, there was nothing written on the back to identify the subjects.

"They look so happy," Sara observed.

"I wonder what's in here." Margaret had discovered a small, velvet jewelry case. She opened it carefully, revealing a lovely gold locket. Inside were tiny, individual photos of Corinne and her carbon copy. "We have to find her," reiterated Margaret. "They were obviously very close."

"Yes," Sara agreed, "and it seems that Corinne was happy at one time. I wonder what happened to change her."

Maggie didn't respond. Her attention focused on something else about the locket. She needed more time to figure out what it was about the necklace that ignited her curiosity. "I think Corinne would want to be buried with this, don't you?" she asked.

"Absolutely," Sara agreed. "Let's take it."

Jeff was standing at the door. "Well, ladies, did you find what you were looking for?" As they turned to look up at him, Margaret felt her heart flutter. It had been over two years since she had allowed herself to feel anything when it came to men, but she couldn't help herself. This Detective Dennison, with the engaging brown eyes, broad shoulders, and gentle, but thoroughly masculine manner, stirred within her urges that she had not acknowledged for some time. At that moment, she realized she wanted to get to know him better, but for the time being, she needed to pull herself together.

Addressing him as matter-of-factly as possible, she managed to ask, "Do you have Corinne's personal effects at the station?"

"Yes. Why?"

"We're looking for a key."

"I don't remember seeing a key on the list, but you're welcome to look through her belongings," he responded. "What are you trying to unlock?" Margaret and Sara showed him the door they had discovered inside Corinne's closet and shared their suspicions about it.

"Hum, it does seem strange to lock an attic space, alright. Have you tried to jimmy the lock?"

"No," answered Sara. "We didn't think your department would take kindly to us defacing property."

As Jeff stood, he spotted something across the room that gleamed in the sunbeam pouring through a west-facing window.

"Maybe you won't have to," he said.

He was squinting in the direction of the portrait over Corinne's bed. As he inched closer, his 6-foot frame provided just enough height advantage to spot something shiny tucked into the bottom right corner of the ornate brass frame. He needed to squint to distinguish one brassy finish from the other. Margaret and Sara, who had been kneeling by the trunk, stood to see what he found.

"What is it?" both women chorused in unison.

Placing one knee on the tall bed, he reached across the headboard and retrieved the tiny treasure.

"You found it! That has to be it! How did we miss it?" The friends were talking over each other excitedly. Amused by their childlike animation, Jeff decided to tease them a bit before surrendering the coveted discovery.

"It'll cost you," he announced, playfully hiding the key behind his back.

"Oh, no you don't, Mister!" Sara declared, reaching around him.

"Hand it over, or we'll have to get rough!" Margaret asserted, joining in the frolic. Jeff was holding the prize above his head, letting it dangle just beyond their reach. Of course, he didn't intend to prevent them access, but this spontaneous play was just what they all needed to relieve the tension that had been building since their arrival.

"These hands are registered weapons!" Sara warned, striking her best feigned karate pose.

"Don't forget, I carry a gu…" Jeff started to say, but as the women crowded him, his foot slipped on the area rug that covered shiny, wooden floorboards. As he toppled backward against the bed's satiny comforter, Margaret landed on top of him, and they both slid to the floor amid Sara's gales of laughter. Margaret gained enough advantage to swipe the key from Jeff's precarious grasp, but not without noticing how his well-defined pectorals felt against her own rapidly beating chest.

"Okay, okay, I give up!" he gasped, with hands in the air. "I'm outnumbered and overpowered."

"You're a wise man, Detective Dennison," announced Sara.

"Come on, Sara. Let's try it!" Margaret had already reached the curious little door and was inserting the key into the lock.

"Does it fit?" Sara inquired.

"Perfectly," Margaret announced, pausing just long enough to exhale the deep breath she had been holding. She turned the key slowly, looking at her two cohorts as if to inquire, "Are you ready?"

The door opened with a slight creaking sound, revealing only darkness beyond the entrance. Their eyes would need to adjust before further investigation was possible.

"Bring that lamp closer," Margaret suggested. "Will the cord reach that far?"

"Hold on," Jeff interjected, reaching into his pocket. "I wasn't a Boy Scout for nothing." From his pocket, he pulled a Swiss army knife. Attached to it was a small flashlight.

"If I ever get lost in the woods," Sara remarked, "I want you with me."

Jeff handed the light to Margaret who shone it into the opening. Illuminating the space revealed nothing more than an empty cavern with rafters running the length of the west wing. An old brick chimney from the fireplace below intersected the sloping roofline, but no hidden treasures greeted the searchers. Margaret's face fell visibly as she backed away from the opening and sat on the floor in defeat. She had felt so sure that the answers to her many questions about Corinne lay behind that locked door, but at that moment, it seemed she would never find them.

"Come on. Let's get out of here," she said, with disappointment filling her voice. Leaving the door ajar, she rose and moved toward the bed to retrieve the funeral garments. She and Sara had abandoned the flashlight on the closet floor, leaving it to Jeff to reclaim and close the attic door. Disheartened, Margaret concluded that they were also leaving behind all hope of finding Corinne's sister and discovering who murdered the twins' mother.

"Wait. What's this?" Jeff cried. He had leaned into the opening for one final look when he spotted something just beyond the miniature doorway. It was propped against the inner wall, between the studs. "It's a book," he announced, answering his own question.

Margaret dropped the clothing on the floor as she and Sara spun around to view the discovery. "I knew it! I knew there had to be something behind that locked door!" she cried, rushing to grab the book from Jeff's hand. Bound in brown leather, it smelled like a well-worn wallet. Across the front, in gold lettering was inscribed the word "Journal." Dropping cross-legged to the floor, Margaret clutched the diary to her chest.

"We don't even know if it's Corinne's journal," Sara warned. "It could have been hidden in that attic for forty or fifty years."

"Given the lack of cobwebs, I doubt it, but there's one way to find out," Jeff prompted, as he sidled close enough to read over Margaret's shoulder.

"Okay. Here goes." Margaret slowly opened the journal to the first page. She couldn't believe her eyes! The first entry was addressed, "Dear Margaret."

A trio of jaws dropped in unison. Leafing through the book confirmed that every entry started the same way and was signed, "Your devoted Corinne." What did it mean?

"Why would Corinne write letters to me? She hardly gave me the time of day, and when she did speak to me, the conversation nearly always ended in a disagreement. 'Devoted?' It doesn't make any sense!"

"Listen. It's getting late," announced Jeff. "Let's get out of here. May I interest you ladies in some dinner?"

"How can you think of your stomach at a time like this?" Margaret inquired, astonished.

"A 'time like this' happens to be dinnertime, and my stomach gets very ornery when I don't feed it."

"Oh, no! I didn't realize it was so late!" exclaimed Sara, looking at her watch. "Listen, Maggie, we found what we were looking for. We can decide what to do with it later. I have to change and meet Alan in thirty minutes. Jeff, would you mind dropping me at my place?"

Chapter 18

As Jeff drove them across town, Maggie clutched the leather-bound volume like a child cradling a long-awaited Christmas toy. She had wanted to dig into its intriguing pages immediately, but her companions insisted that such an auspicious unveiling required a bit more ceremony.

"I can't believe the two of you discovered evidence that our investigation missed!" Jeff exclaimed. "We opened the closet and looked through the contents of the trunk, but I guess we focused too much attention on the mother's bedroom."

"Evidence? Wait! Do you mean we have to turn Corinne's diary over to the police?" Margaret asked.

"Yes, of course. It could contain clues about the case," he affirmed.

"But the words are obviously intended for *me*. Surely you won't seize it without first allowing me to read *my* letters."

"I didn't say you couldn't read it, but I'll need to turn it over to the Captain first thing tomorrow morning. In the meantime, it must remain in my possession."

"In that case, Detective, you have a dinner date. I refuse to relinquish this diary before I've devoured every word. Do you mind, Sara?"

"Of course not," Sara answered a bit absentmindedly. "You can tell me about it tomorrow. Turn right at the next light, Jeff. It's the second building on your left."

As Sara alit from the cruiser and bade them "good night," Jeff invited Margaret to move to the front passenger seat. Deciding it would make her feel less like a perpetrator, she agreed, allowing him to help her out of the back seat and escort her to the front. Although she considered herself a modern woman—strong and independent—Margaret still appreciated chivalry.

"So, how's Italian?" Jeff asked, as they got underway again.

"Pardon me?" Margaret responded. She hadn't yet shifted her thoughts from the journal. So many questions were swirling around in her head! She could hardly wait to read more and secretly wished she could be alone to proceed immediately.

"Food—Italian food," Jeff clarified. "Do you like it?"

"Oh, sorry. Yes, of course," Margaret answered, trying to tear her focus away from the object in her hand that was both fascinating and frightening.

"Alberto's is just around the corner, and I'm starved! Is that okay?"

Margaret wasn't accustomed to being asked for her preference of restaurants or anything else, for that matter. She found it refreshing. She found this man refreshing. He was comfortable to be with and made her feel that she could be herself in his presence.

"Alberto's is just fine. They have great lasagna."

"Ah! You are a woman after my own heart! Lasagna, it is, Signorina."

As they entered the restaurant, Margaret excused herself to the restroom, but not before overhearing Jeff's request for a private table in a quiet corner. Her initial reaction was offense at what seemed a brazen assumption, but quickly she realized he was merely trying to accommodate her need for a quiet reading spot. Moments later, she found him in the furthermost corner of the dining room. He stood as she approached and held her chair for her. *Ever the gentleman*, she thought, approvingly.

"I have two questions for you, Ms. Monroe," Jeff began.

"Okay, uh, shoot," responded Margaret, haltingly. She wondered where this new line of questioning might lead. She sensed that he was as interested in her as she was in him, but preferred to proceed very slowly. She would allow him to ask anything, she decided, but would not hesitate to let him know if he was getting too personal. There was also the lingering guilt about her impulsive decision to break and enter that made her feel wary.

"First, would you like some wine, and secondly, do you mind if I call you Maggie?"

Relieved, she responded with a sigh and a chuckle. "I would love a glass of Riesling, and no, I don't mind if you call me Maggie."

"Are you laughing at me, Maggie?"

"No, no, I'm laughing at myself. I was preparing for another interrogation and amused myself with my unnecessary apprehension."

"I promise not to cross-examine you this evening, but I fully understand how anxious you are to read Ms. Melton's journal. Shall we order dinner and get started?"

"Thank you. I admit to feeling eager, yet apprehensive, about the contents of this little brown book. I can't imagine what could be written to me in a whole book's worth of letters from someone I barely knew—someone whom I thought disliked me, yet summoned me to her deathbed. It's very unnerving." Just then, the waiter approached their table, and the ordering commenced.

Ned, Maggie recalled, would have said, "The lady will have…" immediately taking charge of the situation and making every decision. This man treated her so differently.

Throughout dinner, the conversation flowed effortlessly. They talked about their respective careers, their families, and their hometowns. She learned that he had been married briefly ("young and foolish" was the explanation given) and that he had sustained a flesh wound in the line of duty as a beat cop. He confessed that it shook his confidence enough that he actually considered leaving the force.

Without sharing too much detail, Maggie told him about Ned. If she appeared standoffish, she wanted him to know why. Jeff seemed genuinely interested in getting to know her, and she was beginning to admit to herself that the interest was mutual. By the time the check arrived, they had begun to forge a relationship that each sensed would continue beyond this evening. It had happened without flattery, flirting, or game playing—the common entrapments of dating. *Of course, technically, this isn't a date*, Margaret reminded herself.

For over an hour, the diners forgot about a certain leather-bound volume that lay on the table between them. Suddenly, Margaret realized her opportunity to explore its contents was slipping away. Who knows how long it would have to remain in police custody? She must read it tonight or forfeit the opportunity; however, the long line at the host's station convinced the pair that it would be discourteous to monopolize their table any longer.

"Hey, do you like Rocky Road?" Maggie asked, as they walked to the car.

"Are you kidding? Who doesn't?"

"Well, I just happen to have a quart in my freezer that hasn't been touched yet. I think our reading assignment will give us enough time to polish it off."

"Ms. Monroe, you are a bottomless pit!"

"Thank you, Officer. I pride myself in my capacity for overindulgence. Of course, as soon as the deed is accomplished, I'll be forced to kick you out. Tomorrow is a work day, after all."

"Deal!"

Chapter 19

Jeffrey Dennison had wanted to be a cop since kindergarten. Both his grandfather and his father had served on the force, and he couldn't imagine any other career choice for himself. His mother tried to discourage him to no avail. From experience, he knew that life was hard for the women who married cops, especially city cops. They worried every single day. Every day that their men returned home unharmed was a good day.

As soon as Jeff graduated from high school, he entered the police academy. He worked hard, excelling in every area of training. The day he received his badge was the proudest day in his dad's life. His entire family and his fiancée attended the ceremony. Six months later, he and Adrienne were married.

Chapter 20

Maggie surprised herself by inviting Jeff to her house. It wasn't her style to be so forward, but instinctively, she discerned that she could trust this man.

"Nice digs!" Jeff observed as Maggie led him through the foyer into her morning room. "Of course, I'd expect nothing less from a designer."

"Thanks. Make yourself at home. I'll get the ice cream," Maggie offered, pointing in the direction of the morning room.

"Do you need any help?" he offered.

"No, but a fire would be nice," she said, motioning to the fireplace. "Do you mind?"

"I just happen to be an expert at building fires…another of my many Boy Scout skills."

"How about some hot tea to go with dessert?"

"Sounds good. Do you have herbal? Caffeine keeps me awake."

Wow! Three for three, thought Maggie as she headed for the kitchen. *Lasagna, Rocky Road, and now herbal tea. I wonder what else we have in common.*

Minutes later, the new acquaintances settled on the floor of her morning room with generous helpings of ice cream and mugs of hot tea spread before them on the coffee table. A soothing fire roared in the fireplace, quickly warming the chilly room as, together, they opened Corinne's diary and began to read.

Entry 1:

Dear Margaret,

Well, here I am living with Mother. I never pictured myself coming back here to live, but of course, it was unavoidable. Mother can't manage by herself any longer, and I can't afford to hire any help. Sometimes she doesn't even know who I am. Other times she seems almost normal. Her habits certainly aren't normal, though! I barely recognized the house. It has deteriorated from neglect. Instead of using Daddy's estate money to keep it up, she has spent the entire fortune on things that she'll never use. It's all part of the illness, I suppose. I tried to convince her to sell some of the antiques to help pay the mortgage, but she became hysterical, so I let it go...for now. I won't be able to keep up with the expenses. I must find a job immediately, but I worry about leaving Mother alone. I wish I could talk to you. I feel overwhelmed and scared.

Your devoted Corinne

As Jeff started to turn the page, Maggie stopped him. "Wait, this doesn't make sense. Corinne makes it sound like we knew each other before she came to Beeston. I had never met her before."

"Let's keep reading," suggested Jeff, placing his hand on hers. "Maybe the answers will come." His hand felt comforting, and she made no effort to remove it.

Entry 2:

Dear Margaret,

I'm sorry I haven't written for over a week. I've been busy job hunting. I finally found a position at a design firm. In order to attend the interview, I had to lock Mother in her room. While she was resting one day, I turned the lock around backwards. It felt cruel, but I was afraid she'd either wander off or hurt her-

self in the kitchen. Once, I caught her trying to cook, and she nearly started a fire. She seems to remember how to paint, so I set her up in her bedroom with her easel, acrylics, and canvases, hoping she would remain engaged in her masterpiece until I returned. I've noticed that, if I don't interrupt her, she will focus on a single activity for a long time without tiring.

Jonathan seems nice enough. He wants me to start work on Monday. What will I do with Mother for eight hours a day?

Your devoted Corinne

"Why didn't she tell me in person about her problems? Maggie asked. "She had several opportunities, but she never even mentioned her mother or her financial issues. I would have tried to help, but she always pushed me away. She must have thought I wouldn't listen."

"Let's keep reading," Jeff interrupted. "Something tells me this diary holds the answers to many of our questions about the mysterious Ms. Melton."

Entry 3:

Dear Margaret,

Beeston is like a dream come true, but it's a dream I can't allow myself to enjoy. I spent my whole first day worrying about Mother. She didn't want me to leave this morning, and I had a hard time convincing her that I'd be back soon. I left a lunch tray for her and programmed her DVD to run her favorite movie repeatedly. Repetitive routine seems to calm her. She finally settled down, and I was able to sneak out of the room and lock the door. I don't know what will happen when she realizes she's locked in her bedroom. I got permission to leave work an hour early each day by working through lunch. As soon as I get a handle on my job, I must research options about care for Mother. I feel so alone!

Your devoted Corinne

When Jeff looked up from the page, Maggie was crying.

"If only I had known! Now I understand why she was so difficult and so distant. If only she had told me what she was going through! I would have tried to help, and now it's too late...for both of them."

Jeff, again, placed his hand gently on hers. It felt warm and strong. "But you didn't know. It's not your fault that she chose to write in a journal instead of sharing her concerns with you face-to-face."

"But why?" Maggie asked, not expecting an answer. "Why did she feel she couldn't speak to me directly? Was I so unapproachable? Did Sara and I make her feel like an outsider? We really tried—at first—to include her, to get to know her, but she kept pushing us away. What else could we have done?"

Jeff reached up and gently wiped a tear from her cheek. He wanted to kiss her. He wanted to hold her in his arms and make the guilt and sadness go away, but he sensed that any perceived advances would only add to her pain and confusion. "Do you want to stop?" he asked.

"No, no, I need to find some answers," Maggie sniffed, standing to retrieve a tissue from the table beside her "Vitamin D" chair. "I'm sorry to be so emotional, but this whole situation has thrown me for a loop."

Stoking the fire helped her regain the composure necessary to face Jeff and continue her anxious examination of Corinne's legacy to her. Resuming her position on the floor beside him, she turned to look him in the eye. "I'm really glad you're with me," she said and meant it.

"I am, too," he responded aloud, but he was thinking, *I never want to be anywhere else.*

Entry 4:

Dear Margaret,

Today is Saturday, a day I'll never forget. Mother slept until 8:00 AM. When I went to check on her, she looked so peaceful that I was tempted to let her sleep longer, but I've learned that routine keeps her content, so I gently woke her. She sat up, fluffed her pillows behind her, looked me straight in the eye, and said, "Good morning, Corinne." Immediately, I could tell she was lucid. Gone were the blank stare, the childlike innocence, and the confusion. Mother was back! Who knew how long it might last?

"I've missed you, Darling. I'm so glad you're here," she said, reaching for my hand and cradling it in hers. "I've been lonely, Corinne."

"I know, Mother, but I'm here now, and I'm not leaving again," I assured her.

"Oh, but you must! You have to finish your education, pursue your career, and...live your life."

"I graduated, Mother, remember?" I reminded her. "...and I found a job, a good job right here in town." She hadn't remembered my graduation or the fact that I've been living on the west coast for more than five years. She wanted to know why she hadn't attended my graduation ceremony. I explained that she had been sick and that I understood why she couldn't be there, but she didn't seem to remember much of anything from the recent past...the years since Daddy died.

She noticed her easel standing in front of the window and wanted to know who painted the lovely still life. I didn't have the heart to tell her it was she. I didn't want to upset her and risk losing whatever time we might have before she, again, retreated into the mental abyss that relentlessly beckoned her. Instead, I told her I painted it while she was sleeping.

We reminisced for nearly an hour. She was like her old self—perfectly normal and rational, except for the memory loss. She even talked about Daddy. She told me the story about how they met...the story that she told us so many times as children. Then, I realized she must be hungry. Although I hated to break the spell, I offered to draw her bath and bring her some breakfast. It was so good to have her back, you know?

I filled the tub and poured in her favorite lemon-scented bath salts before heading downstairs to the kitchen, but before I had finished scrambling her eggs, I sensed that something was amiss.

"Wait! Back up!" exclaimed Margaret, suddenly. She and Jeff had been taking turns reading aloud. "Let me see that. '...The story that she told us...'" she re-read, repeating the word *us*. "That's it!" Maggie cried, standing so abruptly that she nearly knocked her teacup to the floor. "Of course, why didn't I think of that before?"

"Think of what?" Jeff wanted to know.

"The locket! Of course!" she cried excitedly, pacing about the room. It was apparent to Jeff that she was thinking aloud, rather than addressing him.

"What locket? Come on, Maggie. We investigators don't like being kept in the dark."

"Sara and I found a gold locket in the trunk. We thought Corinne would want to wear it—you know, to be buried with it. It's still in my coat pocket." Maggie bolted to the hall closet to re-trieve the velvet jewelry case.

"Look! The initials engraved on the front are 'C. M.' Naturally, I assumed the 'M' stood for Melton, but now I'm won-dering if...of course! These letters were not intended for me at all! They were written to Corinne's twin sister, Margaret!"

"Ms. Monroe, you are a detective in the making," was Jeff's response.

"Now that I think about her final words, it all makes perfect sense!" Maggie continued. "Corinne wasn't calling for me. She was asking for her sister. She didn't think I was her mother; she thought I was her sister, Margaret! Oh, Jeff, we must find her! I need to call Sara! She won't believe...what time is it?"

"Okay, slow down. First of all, we don't know for sure that your theory is correct." Maggie started to interrupt, but Jeff con-tinued. "And secondly, it's nearly midnight."

"Midnight? When did it get to be so late?"

"Actually about two hours ago. Listen, Maggie, we both need to get up early tomorrow. I think we should call it a night."

"We can't stop now! There are still too many unanswered questions! We still don't know who killed Corinne's mother! Are you sure you can't leave the diary with me...just for one more day?"

"I could get in a lot of trouble for withholding evidence."

"What if I admitted to discovering the diary and taking it without your knowledge?"

"Then *you* would be the one in trouble with the Law."

"I know, I know, but..."

"Wait. I have an idea."

"What? What is it?"

"Suppose we continue to act as if we think the letters were intended for you? I think I can get permission for you to read the diary after I submit it into evidence. You could stop by the station after work tomorrow and finish it on the premises."

"Are you sure?"

"I'll arrange it, okay? Now, let's both get some sleep." He had already assumed custody of the diary and was heading for the front door. "I'll see you tomorrow."

"Thank you. You've been great," Maggie said, as she opened the door for him. The night air felt chilly, but refreshing as it drifted past them into the foyer.

"Hey, I'll do just about anything for Rocky Road."

He wanted to kiss her, but not until he felt, with confidence, that she would welcome his advance. He couldn't take the chance of alienating her by moving too fast, so he simply said, "Good night," and walked into the darkness.

Chapter 21

Maggie slept very little that night—what little was left of it, that is. Her thoughts of Corinne and the murder case consumed her, but that wasn't all that kept her awake. She couldn't stop thinking about Jeff Dennison: the way he listened, really listened, when she spoke and the way his hand felt on hers, both gentle and strong at the same time.

As soon as she was sure Sara would be awake, Maggie dialed the familiar number. Sara picked up the phone on the first ring and started firing questions even before Maggie could say, "Good morning." She wanted to know everything—not just about the diary, but also about Maggie's dinner with Jeff.

"Listen, we'll see each other at work in an hour, and I'll fill you in—but I just couldn't wait to tell you one thing!"

"What! Did you read the whole diary? Did Corinne kill her mother?"

"No, we didn't finish, and we still don't know if she did it—but we made a very interesting discovery."

"What? What? Spill it!"

Maggie briefed Sara on her discovery about Corinne's twin and how she was sure Corinne's diary entries were intended for *her* eyes. "Can you go to the police station with me after work today? Jeff is arranging for me to finish reading it there."

"Absolutely! Are the police trying to locate Margaret? The poor thing probably doesn't even know she lost her mother and her sister the same night!"

They agreed to meet for lunch and hung up.

Chapter 22

The office was already abuzz when Maggie walked in at 8:55 AM, but conversations hushed abruptly as she approached each huddled group. *I wonder what they've heard about the case that they feel the need to hide from me*, she thought. *Maybe they think Corinne and I were friends, and they're just trying to spare me from discussing her death.*

At precisely 9:00 AM, Jonathan's secretary came across the intercom to announce "a brief, but important staff meeting."

At 9:30, Jonathan's entire design staff gathered in the large conference room on the third floor. Normally, on a Monday morning, they would be standing around chatting animatedly, but this gathering was quite different. Everyone sat in awkward silence. Jonathan walked in and, without bothering to sit, immediately began addressing the group.

"Ladies and gentlemen, I'm sure you've all heard that one of our designers, Corinne Melton, died Friday evening in an automobile accident."

As Maggie glanced about the room, she noticed that no one appeared surprised or moved in any way, for that matter.

Jonathan continued, "Before we begin a new work week, I think it would be appropriate for us to observe a moment of silence."

All heads bowed dutifully, but Maggie and Sara each perceived that Corinne had been a virtual stranger to all of her co-workers, despite having worked among them for nearly a year. To them, the act of reverence was merely a courtesy to their supervisor.

After about a minute (that seemed more like five), Jonathan's "thank you" broke the silence, and he continued by announcing tentative plans for a memorial service later in the week. "As soon as the arrangements are confirmed, I'll share the details with you. I will close our department so that you can attend, if you wish. At present, the police have not been able to locate any next of kin, so the service might be delayed. I'll keep you informed."

"Perhaps you've also heard that Corinne's mother was found dead the same night. I really don't have any information to share with you except to say that a murder investigation is underway. If anyone thinks you might have information to help the police with the case, please don't hesitate to come forward. Thank you. You may be excused."

Maggie could hardly wait until lunchtime, when she would be able to bring Sara up to speed concerning Corinne's journal entries. Certainly, Sara was curious how she had figured out the sister's name, but Maggie's dinner "date" with a certain handsome investigator intrigued her even more. It took considerable self-discipline, on both their parts, to refrain from discussion during working hours.

Precisely at noon, both women made a beeline for the stairs. Outside the building, a bright blue sky and fluffy lamb-like clouds greeted them with the portent of spring, but a brisk March wind served as a reminder that winter still held sway. They strode to a nearby café, hoping their co-workers had opted for the cafeteria.

Over chicken salad wraps and iced tea, Maggie updated Sara on the case, and they agreed to meet at the police station after work.

"That is, unless you and Jeff would prefer privacy," Sara teased. "I don't want to get in the way of a budding romance."

Maggie knew Sara was baiting her, but she didn't mind. It kept the romance talk from getting too serious. Her hedging wasn't a deliberate attempt to withhold information from her best friend. Rather, she needed more time to examine her feelings about Jeff before she could articulate them, even to Sara.

"Just tell me one thing, mi amiga. Did he kiss you?" Sara pressed.

"If and when Jeff Dennison kisses me, you will be the first— make that the second—to know. Deal?"

"Deal."

"Would you have let him?"

"What is this, high school?"

"Okay, I get the message. Case closed...for now."

Chapter 23

Adrienne and her mother sat beside the pool, sipping mimosas. They were determined to finish their frustrating task before lunch. If the invitations were to arrive at their destinations on schedule, they would need to be in the mail by Monday. How could mother and daughter possibly pare the guest list to 300, as Adrienne's father insisted? There was still so much to do before the big day, and the bride-to-be was growing testy under the pressure.

Adrienne and Jeffrey had been high school sweethearts, ever since he spotted her across the room in chem lab. She was a vision in pink. The color of her sweater set matched her rosy lips and cheeks, and complemented her sparkling blue eyes. Whenever she turned her head, those long, golden curls seemed to float through the air in slow motion, landing in perfect spirals down her back. He could hardly take his eyes off her and struggled to stay on task. From that day forward, he set about gaining her attention and her favor. By the end of the week, the two sophomores had become an "item," a status that Adrienne Canfield intended to maintain.

Although their backgrounds differed vastly, Jeffrey's good looks and position as captain of the football team attracted Adrienne, and her parents couldn't help liking the personable young man. He may not have been in the same league as his socialite girlfriend, but he instantly charmed even the bluest of bluebloods. He could learn any social graces that might be lacking, Adrienne determined, and she was just the person to groom him.

Not that Adrienne particularly cared about the differences in their social positions. In fact, to Jeff's amazement, she seemed unaffected by her parents' wealth. To her, affluence was simply a way of life—the only life she knew. The Canfields had worked hard to make sure their children treated others with respect, regardless of their class, race, religion, or any other perceived difference. Money, they insisted, was only as good as its ability to make the world a better place. Clinton and Jean Canfield could well afford to send their daughters to a private school, but felt strongly that public education was the way to keep their children grounded. They were active in the PTA, band boosters, and athletic boosters, generously supporting every fundraiser. They underwrote, anonymously, an entire wing at the school, including a new gymnasium and a much-needed expansion of the library.

Except during football season, Jeffrey spent every Saturday at Adrienne's house in the Hamptons. When they weren't studying together, they swam in the pool and played tennis or badminton. Nine-year-old Tiffany adored her sister's handsome boyfriend, and Jeffrey became the son that Clinton Canfield had always wanted. Canfield, a publishing tycoon, taught Jeffrey to ride and to sail. Trips to the Canfield's summer home on the coast of Maine always included Adrienne's charming beau.

Jeffrey's parents insisted that their children reserved Sundays for church and family, but they always invited Adrienne to join them. She loved his close-knit family, their cozy Brooklyn home, and Sunday dinners of pot roast and home-baked pies.

Never was there any question whether Adrienne and Jeffrey would marry someday. He had learned to live in her world, and she had convinced even herself that she could be a cop's wife. After high school, she had a hard time with their separation, and after only one year at Brown, she decided to drop out of college. Months before Jeffrey finished at the academy, wedding plans commenced in earnest.

The fairytale wedding took place in August. It was picture-perfect, down to the last detail. Even the weather was ideal, but (as little girls often discover too late) fairytales seldom come true.

After a Caribbean cruise (compliments of Adrienne's grandparents), the couple set up house in a modest apartment in the city only three blocks from the police station. Jeffrey was determined to make it financially without help from Adrienne's family, but his new wife was not accustomed to budgeting or to denial of what she considered life's necessities, i.e. weekly manicures, domestic help, and an unlimited expense account.

The newlyweds began to quarrel—not only about money, but also about Jeff's erratic work schedule. As a rookie, he worked a rotating shift. Adrienne thought she could handle this vastly different lifestyle, but the cramped apartment and lack of social engagements began to gnaw at her. At Jeff's suggestion, she landed a job in retail that only lasted a month. She started spending more time at her parents' place than at home, lunching at the country club and playing tennis. Whenever Jeff had to work the weekend shift, she would stay in the Hamptons. The police force allotted no vacation time that first year, so Jeffrey couldn't join the Canfields on their annual trip to Maine. To assuage his guilt, he encouraged her to go without him.

When Adrienne returned to the cramped apartment, her disillusionment with life as a cop's wife was clearly visible to both of them. Despite a stern lecture from her father and the deep disappointment of both sets of parents, she asked Jeffrey for a divorce. It came as no surprise to her husband. He knew she wasn't happy, and more sadly, he knew he was powerless to change the fact.

Jeffrey Dennison was a police officer. He had worked toward that identity his entire life. Any wife of his would have to accept him for who he was, and Adrienne really thought she could manage the role. It turned out that the reality, once thrust upon her, didn't match her fantasy, and it was too late for change.

Youth carries with it endless hope and eternal optimism. Adrienne and Jeffrey had been young and in love. Surely, their love would be enough to guarantee a successful marriage, but their union hardly had a chance to blossom into something enduring. He knew he couldn't give her the desires of her heart, and until then, she hadn't realized how important those desires were to her. They parted amicably, but they parted nonetheless. They would miss each other's families most of all.

Jeff threw himself into work, quickly accomplishing his goal of becoming an investigator. He resumed his education and earned a degree in Criminal Justice. Because New York City footed the bill, he felt obliged to remain on the force for at least the next year. Intrinsically, however, he longed to try the pace of small-town life. The trips to Maine with Adrienne's family had sparked his interest and convinced him that the crimes he might encounter outside the city would be less likely to create a cynical outlook.

Soon he was living in a small town, handling one of the biggest investigations of his career: a double homicide.

Chapter 24

Maggie and Sara left work precisely at 5:00 PM and pulled up to the police station a few minutes later, managing to find two parking spaces directly across from the building. Neither had ever set foot in a police station before, and they felt awkward entering the austere structure that also housed Town Hall. The reception area was quiet with no one in sight. Glancing around the utilitarian office, Maggie observed that it needed a makeover. Some fresh paint and a few fabrics would soften the starkness created by cold metal desks and filing cabinets. On the other hand, she supposed, it was not the function of police stations to make perpetrators feel welcome and comfortable. She was just thinking that she and Jeff should have agreed on a specific place to meet when a middle-aged female officer entered from a room in the back.

"Oh, sorry, I just came on duty. Can I help you?"

"We're here to see Detective Dennison," Maggie answered. "He's expecting us."

"Have a seat," the officer said, motioning toward a wooden bench. "I'll let him know you're here."

"Thanks," answered Maggie and Sara in tandem.

Earlier in the day, Jonathan heard that they were planning to meet Jeff after work, so he gave them Corinne's personnel file to take with them. Maggie resisted delving into the latest details of the case with Jonathan—not because she wished to withhold information, but because she didn't want to be late for her meeting.

She was anxious to see Jeff again. She had thought about him all day and wondered if thoughts of her occupied his mind, too.

The officer was just about to page Jeff when he appeared at a doorway behind the reception desk. "There they are: my two favorite amateur investigators. Sorry to keep you waiting," he said.

"Who are you calling 'amateur,' Mister?" Sara quipped, as both women stood. "We have an entire *day* of sleuthing experience!"

Maggie found herself staring, slightly rattled at the sight of him. His smile was positively unnerving. She couldn't discern whether he might be experiencing a similar reaction, but noticed he seemed to be avoiding direct eye contact as he motioned them toward a hallway to their left.

"Come on back. I have a nice, comfortable interrogation room waiting for you," he said.

He led them past several identically ugly glass-front offices into the bleakest room of all. Surrounded by floor-to-ceiling paneled walls, the only pieces of furniture were a table and two chairs. A single, drab light fixture hung over the table. "Whoa!" exclaimed Sara, "just like in the movies!"

"Sorry it's not more comfortable, but you'll have privacy here." Jeff apologized. "Take your time. My office is just down the hall if you need anything,"

"You're not staying?" Maggie inquired, noticing Corinne's journal on the table.

"I have the forensic reports to review. The results just came back an hour ago, and I haven't had time to look at them. Hey, can I get you ladies a Coke or something? There's a drink machine at the end of the hall."

"I'm fine," answered Maggie, anxious to get started where they had left off the night before.

"Some bottled water would be great," Sara responded.

"Coming right up," Jeff called, as he headed for the door.

"Okay, make it two," Maggie added, suddenly realizing she was parched.

The two women didn't even notice when Jeff returned and placed the bottles of water at their elbows. They were already engrossed in the journal, eager to learn more about the mysterious Corinne Melton and her elusive twin sister.

Chapter 25

"Here's where we left off last night," Maggie was explaining to Sara. "This is where I realized Corinne's sister must be named Margaret."

Entry 4, continued:

Usually, I can hear water splashing in the tub when Mother bathes, and often she sings the lullabies that she sang to us as children, but it was quiet upstairs—too quiet. An ominous foreboding engulfed me. I abandoned her breakfast tray and ran up the stairs. Thank God I arrived when I did!

I found Mother in her dressing gown, sitting on the window seat. She was staring at her easel with a pistol in her hand. I wanted to scream, but was afraid of what she might do if I startled her. I didn't know if the gun resting on her lap was loaded or where she had found it. I thought Mother sold Daddy's entire collection after he died. She seemed dazed until I began to approach her slowly, carefully. I wasn't sure if she was cogent or not. Would I be able to reason with her? Could our gentle, nurturing mother actually be dangerous?

"You were right, Maggie! This diary was intended for Corinne's sister! But where is she, and why did Corinne keep a journal instead of writing directly to Margaret? Better yet, why didn't she pick up the phone and call her, not to mention e-mail and texting? This is the twenty-first century, after all!" Sara was gesturing wildly as she always did when she became excited. "I know! I know!" answered Maggie. "Keep reading!"

As I began speaking quietly, her gaze shifted from the painting to me, and she spoke soberly. Her voice was calm and steady. Her eyes reflected perfect reason. "It's better this way, Corinne. I know what's happening. I know I'm going insane, just like my mother. Let me do this while I can still think clearly. Let me make this choice for us—for you. It'll be better for both of us, darling."

"Mother, what are you saying?" I asked, trying to remain calm, but I knew exactly what she meant to do. I needed to stay composed—to inch closer without her noticing. I needed to keep her talking. My heart was beating out of my chest, and I felt beads of sweat forming on my forehead, but somehow I managed to engage her in conversation about Daddy and got her thinking about how he would want us to stay together. I told her about my job and that I would be able to take care of us. I told her I wouldn't leave her. I assured her she could stay in her home, and I would take care of her the way she had always taken care of us.

Finally, I drew close enough to grab the gun from her, but she had already raised it to her head. Then, instantly, she was gone. Our dear mother disappeared as suddenly as she had surfaced earlier. I hid the weapon under my shirt until I could find a way to dispose of it. Gently, I led the docile child, Agatha, to the bathroom and helped her finish her bath.

Later, I removed the lone bullet and placed the gun under lock and key in our secret play space under the eaves. She would never have access to it again, but I had no way of knowing where she had found it in the first place and whether there were others in the house.

"This proves Corinne's innocence, Sara!" Maggie exclaimed. "Agatha Melton tried to kill herself before, and Corinne actually saved her life. She must have found another of her husband's guns. Yes, Jeff said the weapon was registered to Robert Melton."

"You were right, Maggie! Corinne's mother committed suicide! Her diary proves it!"

"Keep reading!" Maggie urged.

Thankfully, the next day was Saturday, and I could be with Mother all day. I can't predict what her state of mind will be from one day to the next. First thing Monday morning, I'll start looking for someone to stay with her while I'm at work.

Your devoted Corinne

Entry 5:

Dear Margaret,

A week has passed since I've had time to write. I've been so busy! I've spent hours researching potential caregivers for Mother. I'm afraid my work is suffering, but I must find someone soon. I discovered that Mother's insurance will cover the cost of home healthcare, but the local agency doesn't have anyone available at the present time. I can't keep leaving work early, or I'll lose my job. My co-workers are already becoming suspicious and irritated with me, but leaving Mother alone for more than a few hours simply is not an option. I miss you so much, Margaret!

Your devoted Corinne

Entry 6:

Dear Margaret,

I can't spend another weekend cooped up in this prison! Our bedroom is my sanctuary, but even here, especially here, the memories threaten to overtake me, and I must flee them. Now that winter is upon us in earnest, we spend our evenings in the den. Mother watches her favorite programs, and I read or try to stay caught up with my projects at Beeston. I wonder if Mother and Daddy had any friends. Surely, they must have. Perhaps their friends deserted them when you left us. I don't remember. I choose not to remember.

Your devoted Corinne

Entry 7:

Dear Margaret,

I think you'll like what I've done to our room. I had to clear the clutter and make some changes or go crazy. I spent three entire weekends stripping that God-awful flowered wallpaper, and yesterday, as Mother rocked one of her dolls and sang lullabies, I painted the walls yellow—cowslip yellow. I think a cowslip is a flower.

You remember, of course, the French writing desk that Mother bought for a pittance at a yard sale when we were children. The poor souls that sold it to her never suspected what they possessed. It must be worth a fortune now, but to me it is simply an object of great beauty. Mother helped me move it from the third floor to a place of honor in our bedroom between the windows. She may be losing her mental acuity, but she's still as strong as an ox.

The third floor is just as it was when we used to take in lodgers—furniture and all. I don't know when Mother had it boarded up. I suppose the care of so many rooms became too much for her. It took nearly an hour for me to remove the barrier. I thought Mother would object, but she was particularly docile that day. She did make me promise to replace the boards when I finished "…to lock away the memories," she said. Next weekend, I'll look through her vast collection of fabrics for some cheerful window treatments. I wonder if she remembers how to sew.

Your devoted Corinne

"I took the liberty of ordering pizza," Jeff announced. The intent readers hadn't even noticed when he appeared at the door of the interrogation room. "I hope you like pepperoni."

"You're a saint, Detective. I'm starved!" Sara responded.

"Corinne didn't murder her mother, Jeff! She committed suicide! I'm sure of it! She adored her mother!" Maggie cried, excitedly. "Mrs. Melton had tried to kill herself before! It's all right here in…"

"I know," Jeff interrupted. "Pizza?"

"What do you mean, you know?"

"I read the journal this morning."

"What? You knew she was innocent, and you didn't say anything?" Maggie blurted.

Sara had already helped herself to a huge bite of the mouthwatering pizza, but suddenly stopped chewing. If a lovers' first quarrel was about to erupt, she didn't want to miss a single word.

"I had to wait for the forensics reports to be sure—to have actual proof, but the diary certainly confirms that Corinne loved her mother and that Mrs. Melton had tried to kill herself before," Jeff said. "I sent an officer to the house to look for the gun mentioned in the diary. He found it in the attic just beyond the chimney."

"You knew all of this and didn't say anything?" Maggie asked, sounding irritated.

"Wouldn't you have wanted to finish the diary, anyway?" queried Jeff. "…And, like I said, I still needed material evidence to close the case."

"You're right, of course," Maggie resolved, lowering her hackles. "But what about the report?"

"The fingerprints were unidentifiable, but there was only one set of DNA on the handle of the weapon: Agatha Melton's."

"I knew it!" Maggie cried, standing. "Corinne must have been consumed with fear and grief when she ran from the house that night! Of course, she blamed herself!" Maggie was pacing, recalling Corinne's final words to her in the hospital. "She thought I was her sister, Margaret, and she wanted me to go to their mother. She was looking for Margaret when she ran off the road and hit a tree!"

Maggie was crying. Jeff rushed to her and cradled her head against his chest.

"She was so alone!" Maggie sobbed. "Forgive me, Corinne. I didn't know how you were suffering!"

Although Maggie and Jeff had become unaware of Sara's presence, she tiptoed out of the room, with tears welling in her eyes. She, too, shared Maggie's guilt at not sensing their co-worker's plight, but deep down, she understood that Corinne would never have let them get close enough to share her struggle. There was nothing more that they could have done because Corinne had been determined not to let anyone into her miserable life.

Sara's tears were as much for her friend as for Corinne—a mixture of sadness and joy. She realized that Maggie had fallen in love—finally, completely head-over-heels in love. Somehow, she understood (as only a best friend can) that Jeff Dennison was the man who would heal her wounded heart and cherish her forever.

Chapter 26

The double service at Abbott's Funeral Home was, of necessity, generic. So little was known about the deceased mother and daughter that any attempt at a eulogy would have been forced, so the minister simply read some appropriate Scriptures and recited a couple of prayers.

Although the home at 220 Monument Avenue had sheltered only the Melton family for more than thirty years, none of the original neighbors remained. The current residents knew nothing about the home's occupants except for rumors of a crazy woman who talked to herself and sometimes appeared on the front porch in her underwear. According to the police investigation, the neighbors, who deliberately avoided the house, conjectured that she had either become bedridden or passed away years ago. The young woman who moved in last year was a caretaker, they assumed.

The remainder of Corinne's diary provided a window into the private life of the young woman who had presented herself so differently in public. It confirmed her lonely existence of the last year and her devotion to her mother, but it failed to answer the ardent question that lingered in the minds of Maggie and Sara. Where was Margaret Melton, and why had she not surfaced following the deaths of her mother and sister?

Jeff's investigation had finally tracked down a cousin of Robert Melton living in Indiana. Because of health concerns, the woman was unable to travel for the service; however, she related, by telephone, that Agatha Relsford Melton, abandoned at an early age, had spent her childhood in the foster care system. She recalled a vague account of her birth mother's commitment to a psychiatric institution, but couldn't confirm its legitimacy. Robert, she said, had once confided that Agatha never spoke of her childhood, not even to him, claiming that her life began when she married him.

The cousin also shed light on the mystery concerning Corinne's twin sister, but Jeff would wait until just the right moment to share that information with Maggie. In the meantime, a visit to Robert Melton's grave was in order.

Chapter 27

Jonathan encouraged his staff of fourteen to attend the funeral, and they obliged dutifully. Adorning each casket were lovely matching sprays of pink roses and baby's breath, sent by Beeston Enterprises. Jonathan also requested that Maggie and Sara sit on the front row. They accommodated his appeal—not because either felt justified in occupying seats normally reserved for family, but because, sadly, there was no one else. Flanking the women were Alan and Jeff. Maggie and Sara held hands and wept silently—not so much for lost lives as for opportunities missed.

A day earlier, Jeff had invited Maggie to ride with him to the cemetery. Assuming he needed her help in selecting a burial plot, she agreed to meet him after work. As they approached the iron gated entrance, Jeff stopped the car. "Let's walk from here," he suggested. "There's something I want you to see."

It was the warmest spring afternoon thus far. Without the ample canopy of trees flanking both sides of the gravel path, it might have proven uncomfortably warm. The days were growing longer now, and Maggie relished the extra hours of daylight. Usually, it meant that she could tackle her flowerbeds after work each day—except for this week, of course, in which she had spent every afternoon otherwise engaged. Not that she minded seeing Jeff on a daily basis—on the contrary, she was beginning to realize that a day without seeing him felt incomplete. It had happened so easily, so naturally—this budding friendship—that she hadn't even considered trying to thwart it...nor did she resist his hand as it reached for hers.

Only a pleasant harmony of birdcalls interrupted the stillness of this place. *How peaceful it is here*, Maggie thought. *If I were a bird, I would choose to nest here, too.* How perfectly manicured the grassy areas were! How refreshing to be greeted by real flowers rather than those gaudy plastic or silk bouquets that affronted most cemeteries! She made a mental note to inform any of her future progeny to allow no artificial flowers at her gravesite.

The couple walked some distance in silence, each sensing that such reverent stillness should remain devoid of human chatter. Looking around at the gravestones imbued Maggie with a sense of connection to the universe. Each represented a life lived, dreams dreamed, and history played out. Some engravings attested to long, fruitful lives. Many, especially before 1900, paid tribute to lives abbreviated by who-knows-what disease or battle, but Maggie couldn't help thinking that all who laid at rest in this place—and millions of similar places—were connected by a common humanity. *How ironic that, in such a spot as this, I feel my life just beginning*, she thought.

They strode far enough into the park-like setting that the front gate was no longer visible, finally stopping at a fenced-in family plot. It rested atop a slightly elevated knoll, surrounded by a grove of mature pecan trees. No flowers adorned this area. There in the center stood a marble tombstone about Maggie's height. It bore the inscription, "Robert Norris Melton, loving husband and father, 1939–1999."

On one side of the central marker were two gravesites, obviously reserved for future use. A small, plain stone marker identified each. On the far side, Maggie could see another tombstone, but couldn't make out the words. She didn't need to do so. Suddenly, she understood why Jeff brought her there.

As she approached the simple gravestone, sparkles of sunlight glittered through the tree canopy and danced a gigue upon the shiny granite. Maggie squinted hard, willing her eyes to adjust to what she now realized the ornate etching would reveal—the final missing piece to the puzzle of Corinne Melton's life. She read it aloud.

"Margaret Anne Melton, 1967–1982: much loved; forever missed."

During the graveside ceremony the following day, Maggie noticed a middle-aged man standing apart from the sparse gathering. Assuming he was a funeral home employee, she quickly dismissed his presence as insignificant—that is, until the group began to disperse. Glancing toward the knoll one last time, she spotted the man, smartly dressed in a navy blue Armani suit, crisp white shirt, and burgundy tie. As the others walked toward their waiting cars, he lingered at the open grave, and curiously, discreetly, he dropped a single red rose into the crevasse that would soon swallow Corinne's simple brown casket. Was Maggie the only one who overheard his mournful murmur? "Rest in peace, my love," he said.

"Rest in peace, Corinne," she whispered and departed with Jeffrey Dennison at her side.